BORN IN THE APOCALYPSE BOOK 3
"JERICHO"

JOSEPH TALLUTO

SEVERED PRESS
HOBART TASMANIA

BORN IN THE APOCALYPSE 3

CHAPTER 1

"No one who ever went over ever came back."

Those words were the only thing I could think of as I stared up at the expanse of concrete in front of me. I put a tentative hand out to the wall, not really believing it, then jerked my hand away as I realized it truly was there and I was on the wrong side of it.

Every story I had ever heard about the other side of the wall came flooding back. Everything my dad had ever told came right to the front of the line of my imagination. Hordes of Trippers, devastated cities, survivors running scared ahead of the Trippers, fortified towns falling to teeth and nails.

All of the scenarios that played out in my head at that moment had me reaching a single conclusion: I was a dead man.

I took stock of what I had, and the list wasn't great. I had my Colt, my knife, and a few gold and silver coins hidden in my gun belt. I had the clothes on my back, and my hat. That was it.

"How in the name of all that's Holy do I get back there?" I asked myself aloud, stepping back to look at the wall. The land was clear directly in front of the edifice, and there were no trees that grew within fifteen feet. The grass was low and even, like it was cut specifically to keep it low. That struck me as very odd, and I bent down to take a look at the grass. The edge of the blades was severed neatly, and as I ran my hand through the grass, small pieces jumped up in the air. That was weird. This grass had been cut, and recently.

None of that made sense. Why the heck would anyone want to keep grass a certain height, and more importantly, who would waste time cutting grass near a wall? The Trippers would be all over anything like that. Maybe it was cut a long time ago and just stayed this height. Right now, that was the only thing I could think of.

I looked at the wall of trees and brush ahead of me, and realized that was probably my best hope for survival. Trippers didn't do all that great with brush and trees, not typically looking where they walked. I grabbed up my hat and ducked into the woods.

I knew the outer brush would not be the same once I got under the canopy. That was the first thing my dad taught me about the woods. They usually looked like they were impenetrable, but once you got past the outer edge, the brush under the trees was usually very thin.

It was the same here. The trees were young, but old enough to cross limbs and create an overhead blanket of green. The trees were probably fifteen to twenty years old. That green was turning red, brown, and yellow, but I didn't have time to admire the view. My thoughts were strictly survival right now. I needed to find some kind of secure place to spend the night. I needed to find a source of food, and a source of water. Right now, I had no idea where to find any of that. I could create a shelter from the trees, but no Tripper would be stopped by it. I could sleep up in the trees, but I ran the risk of waking up to a rather unpleasant breakfast committee. My best bet right now was to keep going, and hope I might come across some kind of shelter or house or something. I mean, the world had towns and cities before the Trippers came in Illinois.

I had gone for about fifty yards in the woods when I heard a strange sound behind me. It was a buzzing noise, like a wasp stuck inside a drain pipe. It faded and expanded, and reached both a high pitch and then a low one. I froze in place, not knowing what that sound was. But as I listened, it seemed like it was flying above me.

I stayed put, keeping myself pressed up against a tree with my head level. I was grateful my coat was dark and my hat was, too.

Something flew overhead, and before I realized it, I had my hand on my gun. Whatever it was, it sounded angry and dangerous. I waited for a long time, and I was never more grateful than I was at that moment that my father had taught me to be a patient hunter. I could wait for hours, and since I had no idea what sort of nastiness was flying around, I wasn't going to move.

A few minutes later, the buzzing seemed to move away towards the east, and I was glad to see it gone. I had never heard of anything like that before, and I certainly did not want to meet it again. My head filled with strange ideas, like giant wasps and other things, but not even in my imagination could I figure out what that might have been.

I moved on, going deeper into the woods. The trees were mostly maple, with a few oak tossed in here and there for good measure. I thought I saw a couple of fruit trees, but I wasn't sure. One thing I did notice as I moved was the trees seemed to grow in rows. That was extremely odd. I had never seen that before, and I had been in a number of woods.

I looked back over my shoulder and I couldn't see the wall anymore. For some reason, that bothered me. It felt like I was getting too far away from my home. I didn't want to get too far away from the wall, but there was nothing there that could let me survive the night. I needed to move before nightfall, and find a place to survive in.

As I walked on, I saw a clearing on my left. I went over in that direction, hoping to have a chance to get my bearings. I knew I was going east, but if I could get up a little higher, I could see if there was some sort of shelter I could head for. I pushed through the brush as quietly as I could, hoping that whatever it was that had buzzed over my head would not be able to track me by sound.

When I reached the clearing, I paused, looking around like I always had, looking for traces of passage, anything that didn't fit with the rest of the picture. I didn't see anything along the edge of the clearing, so I stepped carefully out. I could hear birds arguing in the branches, and I thought I saw the grey flash of a squirrel. I kept my head down, and moved out, keeping to the edge of the clearing. The grass was tall in the center, and I was a bit curious as to why there weren't any trees growing here.

About a quarter of the way around, the ground I stepped on suddenly snapped. I looked down and didn't see any twig, so I lifted my boot and saw a flash of white under the grass. I had seen enough of them to know one when I saw it. I had just stepped on a bone.

I reached down, and as I got lower, I could see the ground was lumpy and uneven, rising as it got closer to the center. I scraped away some more of the ground, and unearthed several more bones. I had seen enough Tripper action in my life to know when I was looking at human bones. The more I looked around the clearing, the more I was convinced this wasn't a clearing at all. It was a burial ground.

I stepped back into the brush and worked my way toward the other side of the clearing. I didn't want to step on or disturb any more of the grave.

On the other side of the clearing, I passed back into the woods, and I stepped on something else that cracked. It sounded hollow, so I looked down again. This time, I had stepped on a skull. But this skull was not like any I had ever seen that had been taken down by a Tripper. This skull had a neat hole right in the center of it. I stepped away, and as I did, I looked back. I couldn't help but think I was looking at more of a killing field, not a burial ground.

I moved on, not hearing that buzzing sound anymore, following the trees as they flowed away from the way. I looked at the sky and figured I had about four hours before things started heating up. I needed a place to settle in and fast, or I was going to have to spend the night up in a tree or buried in the ground. I had to do that once, and it was the worst sleep I ever had, breathing into my hat as Trippers wandered around.

I walked for what seemed to be several miles, and the sun dipped further along its path. The woods were full, yet as I walked, there were other clearings I saw on my left and right, but I didn't bother to explore. I had a feeling I would find the same thing as I did in the first clearing.

Through the trees I spotted something, something that didn't look like a tree or its neighbor, and keeping low, I headed over towards it. From the glances through the trees, it looked like a building. I didn't care if it was a shack with the sky for a roof, it was shelter, and I was grateful for it.

I stepped out of the brush and looked at the building. It was a small garage, detached from the house that was a few yards further away. The house and garage looked like they had been abandoned for years, and as I looked closer, it seemed like the family that used to be here had left like they had planned on returning. The house was empty of furniture, at least I couldn't see any from the windows. I tried the doors, but they were locked tighter than I cared to try right now. The sun was below the horizon and it was getting darker by the minute.

I cracked the door on the garage and slipped inside, making sure to close it tightly once I was inside.

It was hard to see, but there was enough light coming in to make out the big shape of the car still inside, as well as the shelves of containers and boxes. I would look a little deeper in the morning to see if there was anything I could use to get me back over the wall.

I opened the car and slipped into the back seat. As I took off my gun and knife, I suddenly realized how tired I was. I lay down and was almost asleep immediately. I woke once, thinking I heard another buzzing sound, but I couldn't hear it again, so I figured it was just a residual memory.

My last thoughts before drifting off to sleep were about Kim and the horses. I hoped they made it back to the houses okay and didn't try to stick around.

CHAPTER 2

In the morning, I went over the stuff left in the garage, but didn't find anything of use. I was hungry, but I had been there before, and the view wasn't any different this time. I would eat what I could find, and if not now, later.

Outside, the world was bright and green, and as I was able to see better, I could discern a number of buildings in the trees.

"That's not right," I said aloud. I walked carefully outside, and as I looked around, I had a hard time believing what I was seeing. There was a neighborhood right in the middle of the forest. There were rows of houses down what was now an obvious street. The grass had grown over the roadway, but it was still easy to see where the road was. Trees were growing thickly in every yard, and there were even trees growing in the middle of the road. I walked over to the next house, and found it similar in condition to the one I had just left. I tried the door on this one and was slightly surprised to find it open.

Inside, the house was mostly empty, but I did manage to find some dried oats in a can. I realized suddenly and clearly I had no water. As soon as I focused on that, I was instantly thirsty. I forced the slight panic I felt down, having no room for it in my plans for today. I went through the rest of the house, and managed to find a small satchel, two small boxes of matches, a candle, and some twine. It wasn't much, but I felt like I was halfway home after finding these things.

Back outside, I went to the next house, and kept up the pattern all the way down the block. The homes were the same, pretty empty except for a few things here and there, and I added to my survival kit as I went along. I had a brief moment of brilliance when I thought I could just grab some ladders and get up the wall that way, but my moment to shine was over when I discovered that none of the homes I visited had ladders. Not a single one.

The best thing I discovered was a small pocketknife that had a lot of folding features. I didn't need it right now, but I appreciated the screwdrivers, and the little scissors. Sometimes the easiest way to get through a locked door was to pop the hinge pins.

I stopped going into homes after a bit and kept heading east. I knew what was west, and east seemed to be the easiest route to take. I moved through what used to be a downtown area, but the businesses were all closed up, and there were trees growing right in the middle of the center traffic stop. It slowly dawned on me that there was no way trees would grow in the middle of an intersection. There was only one way they had gotten there and that meant they had to have been planted. When I reached that conclusion, things started falling into place. Empty homes, no signs of violence, trees planted all over the place, no Tripper activity anywhere. Everyone had left this place willingly, and they planted trees to cover their tracks. But why trees? Who could see anything except from a high place?

None of it made sense to me, and I started to think that the Trippers may have died off out here, making is safe for the rest of us to come out. That was a happy thought. We could gather everyone out of the state, and lock the Trippers in.

That fantasy moved me along, and I followed the road that lead out of town. It wasn't a road in the strict sense of things, just a cleared area in the grass. But it was straight and lead east, which was where I wanted to go.

About an hour later, I found a small stream winding its way through the woods, and by the look of it, it had been there for a very long time. I took a long drink, then filled a bottle I had found in one of the houses.

The woods stretched out for miles, and I was interested to see how far it went. If I had my horse, I would have explored this more thoroughly. Thinking of Judy refocused my thoughts on getting back home, and how I was going to do that.

The empty woods gave me a lot of time to think, and I realized that the wall had openings, I just had never explored them fully. I didn't need a rope or a ladder, I just needed to be able to cut through one of the bars that blocked the waterways. I could just follow the wall until I got to the lake, and get in from there.

I didn't bother to think about the fact that when I did get through, I would be in the heart of a city full of Trippers. Why burden myself with details?

I walked on, and found myself going through another town. This one was like the last one, with empty homes and businesses, and trees planted where there shouldn't be trees. I went into a number of garages and homes, looking for foodstuffs, mostly, but keeping my eye out for a hacksaw.

I found one finally, and stored in my bag. I also found a length of rope, which I stored as well. That was my backup plan. If way leads to way, then I would need the rope as a last means to get over the wall.

This town had an oddity the last one didn't, though. In the business section of town, every building that was over two stories had been leveled at the second story. The broken pieces were piled up against the buildings, giving the grass a hill to grow against. Taken with my observations before, I made the guess that these buildings were meant to be hidden under the trees. The 'what' was easy to figure out, but the 'why' eluded me.

I think I walked for another good couple of hours, and stopped suddenly. The woods I was walking through ended abruptly, and on the other side there was a straight road. Something told me not to try crossing that road during the day, so I tucked myself up under a bush, covered my face with my hat, and went to sleep.

In the last light of the day, I woke, and long experience sleeping outdoors had taught me not to move until I had measured my surroundings. I heard no wheezing, no steps through the underbrush, and there was a good collection of birdsong around me. I slipped my hand up slowly and took my hat off my face. I slipped out of the brush and took a quick look around. The woods were dark, but there was nothing dangerous nearby.

I stepped out onto the road, and a quick look told me it went out of sight both north and south. On the other side of the road was another fence, this one was just chain link, but it was tall enough that any Tripper would never get over it. On the other side of the road was open field. As I looked through the fence, I could see lights moving in the distance, within a larger grouping of lights.

My mind raced back to that day when I first saw the lights, when Trey and I were holed up in a tall building.

I had to know what those were, if only for my own sanity. I had read of will-o-the-wisps and a superstitious part of me wondered if I was seeing something of that nature here. Who was to say that if mankind left the earth, would magic that may have been dormant suddenly rise again?

I scaled the fence and was over in a few seconds, slipping into the heavy grasses. I walked carefully, keeping a hand on my knife and gun. I couldn't explain it, but I didn't feel as if there were Trippers nearby.

I was about a quarter-mile from the road when I heard it. It came from the north, and approached quickly. I ducked into the grass and looked back, trying to see what made the noise. It was a dull roar, and grew louder as it came closer. In the grey light, I could see a car approaching, moving in the dark. Its lights were out, but it stayed on the road without difficulty. As it passed, I could see the driver's pale face staring out into the darkness. I could have sworn as he went by he looked out the window and stared right at me. I didn't move, I just stayed where I was, like a deer hoping immobility would serve as camouflage.

I tried to absorb what I had seen, and finally figured it was someone who still had a working car, and kept the lights out so as not to attract Trippers. The sound would carry and that might bring any within hearing to investigate, so I figured I'd better get moving.

I stayed low in the grass, keeping an eye on the lights to the east. I could see a few moving now, and it was fascinating to watch. I realized as I watched them that they were cars, moving as if there wasn't a Tripper for miles. I had to wonder if there was a fence I couldn't see or some other kind of barrier. I kept my eyes open for a pit or some other obstruction. I had to find some place to spend the night; I didn't want to approach this place in the dark.

Off to the south, I saw a dark, box-like shape, so I made my way over to it. It was a small, two-story farmhouse, and it looked like it had seen better days. The trees and grass grew right up to it, and I had to pull a large pine branch out of the way of the door to get it open. Inside the house was bare and dusty, but the windows and doors were secure, so I knew I could rest here tonight. I went upstairs and locked myself in a small room.

CHAPTER 3

In the morning, I went downstairs, and spent some time looking over the house. It was a simple affair, made to seem larger with wide windows. I could see some of the fields outside through the trees and shrubs, and on a whim, I went back upstairs and looked out towards the east. I could see the town in the distance, and even in the early light, I could see cars moving and people moving around. I watched for a long time, and saw no towers, no guards, no defense whatsoever. Maybe the fences I had climbed earlier were keeping the Trippers away, and I had managed to come through without seeing any.

I took a look out the west window, and off in the distance, I could see a grey line right above a green one. I knew I was looking at the wall, and I couldn't help but feel a pang to get back over there.

I looked to the south and noticed something red on the side of the building. It looked like some kind of writing. I couldn't see it clearly, so I went outside and fought the brush to the west side of the building.

Up on the second floor, someone had painted in large red letters: JARED HUTCHINS WE ARE SAFE COME HOME.

I had no idea what to make of that. I looked west and tried to judge the distance. I figured someone with a really good riflescope might just make out the letters if they were high enough.

I tossed that one over in my head as I started walking over to the town. Experience had taught me to stash my Colt in my satchel. It was out of sight but with a flip of my hand I could get it out quickly enough.

The town looked normal enough; I had seen enough of them to know when they were occupied. But this one blew away my expectations by miles. The streets were clean, no signs of violence, and the occasional car drove by. No one was walking on the streets that I could see, but I was trying to take in as much as I could. Every business was occupied, although only a few were open. A small restaurant was open, and as I passed, I could smell fantastic things coming from that place, things I hadn't eaten since my mother died years ago. I couldn't stop myself; I turned and walked into the place.

There were two people sitting at the counter, and I took a stool on the far edge. I wanted to be able to see the door and the rest of the place. I took off my hat and placed it on the counter in front of me.

"Coffee, cowboy?" a voice spoke in front of me.

I turned to see an older woman standing on the other side of the counter, holding a pot of coffee. I nodded, and she filled a nearby cup.

"Get you something to eat?" she asked. She looked like she had seen a few long roads herself. Her hair was pulled back in a severe bun, held in place by a pink bandana. Her face would have been pretty a long while back, and she had weary blue eyes. She was probably younger than she looked.

"I'll have some eggs and bacon, thanks," I said. I had never ordered anything before, but I had read about people doing it.

"Sure thing, hon. Like your hat, by the way." The woman walked away and yelled something unintelligible to a hole in the wall. The hole answered with an equally unintelligible noise.

I slipped my hat off to the side as the other men at the counter looked me over with short, quick glances. Whatever they read in their glance must have satisfied their curiosity because they went back to their coffee and breakfasts.

I was trying hard not to stare at everything around me. Nothing I was seeing made any sense. There were no walls, no one was armed, and people seemed to come to this place on a regular basis to simply have breakfast. What did the men at the other end of the counter do during the day? I had no answers, and I wasn't about to ask. I kept my eyes on the counter in front of me and my hands stayed where they were.

Finally, I stared out the window at the town, watching it wake up while I waited for my breakfast. There seemed to be a sense of urgency as people began their days, and more cars began to show up on the roads. I had never seen such a town, and I wondered how they managed to make it all work, especially when I was seeing electricity, gasoline, and natural gas all in good supply. I was starting to feel a bit overwhelmed.

My breakfast came and I dug in. The eggs were scrambled, and there was a lot of them. I ate everything, having not eaten for over a day. The bacon was fantastic, something I hadn't had in a very long time. The woman filled my coffee cup three times. The last time she mentioned my appetite.

"Like to see a hungry man eat," she said with a smile.

I nodded around my mouthful of biscuit. "It's been a bit since I ate last," I said.

"You think you have enough?" she asked, looking at my plate.

"I could eat another plate if that's what you're asking," I said, swallowing the biscuit.

"I'll send the order in," she said as she walked over to the small window.

I finished my first plate of breakfast and waited with my coffee for the refill. The men down at the other end of the counter finished their meals and pulled out some bills to pay for their fare.

I suddenly began to panic. I had seen that kind of money before; my dad had shown it to me when I was younger. In Illinois, that stuff was useless for anything other than lighting fires, but it seemed they still used it for commerce here. I had a couple of silver coins with me, inside my gun belt, but I had no idea if they would take that as payment. If I flashed my gold, that might really raise some eyebrows.

My second plate of food arrived, and I decided to ask before I got into trouble. I dug a silver coin out of my pack and placed it on the counter.

"Ma'am? I seem to have left home with nothing but this for payment. Will it do?" I asked.

The woman picked up the coin and looked at it closely.

"One ounce silver," she read on the coin's back. "Huh. Haven't seen any of these for a long time. Not since the trouble. Not sure what it's worth," she said, putting it down. She looked over to a corner of the diner.

"Earl? You got the paper. What's silver worth these days?" She directed her question to an old gentleman having his repast in a corner booth. He flipped through a few pages and ran a finger down a list of something.

"Spot price today is twenty-seven forty-five," the man said, before flipping back to the page he was reading before.

The waitress turned back to me. "You're good, hon. Fact is, I'll owe you some change. Chef said not to charge you for the refill since he's glad he's met a man who likes his cooking."

My panic abated, and I ate easily. When the second plate was finished, I gathered up the paper money and coins left near me and following the lead of the men who had left earlier, I left two single dollar bills on the counter. Gathering up my hat and satchel, I went out onto the street. I had a sated stomach, but my mind was full of hungry questions.

CHAPTER 4

I walked down the street, just taking in the activity and trying not to attract too much attention to myself. There were several men walking about wearing hats similar to mine, so no one gave that a second look. I didn't take my gun out of my satchel, since no one I saw wore a gun openly.

Further into town, there were more people about, and the shops were all full of goods and supplies. I had never seen such a variety of things for sale, and I sent a good portion of the morning slowly walking the street, and looking into windows.

At the end of the block, there was a small store, and the sign outside said it was a pawn shop. I had read about them, but had never seen one in person that was open. A small sign in the window caught my eye, and caused me to open the door and walk in.

The interior was an incredible mix of goods and supplies. Whoever owned this place tried to organize it into themes like electronics, sporting goods, and camping supplies. Despite their valiant efforts, things were spilling over into other areas. I looked over a section labeled "Army Surplus," and I wondered if this was stuff that had been collected when the army was defeated. There were two other men in the store when I entered, and they were over at the counter haggling with the proprietor over some large knives.

The owner looked over at me. "Be with you in a second!" he called.

"No hurries," I said. I went over to the camping supplies and saw a few items that I would like to have with me. An idea came to me. "Do you have any rope?" I asked in the general direction of the counter.

"Around the corner, got some nylon cord," the disembodied voice replied.

I found the rope, and it was just what I was looking for. It was wrapped in a bundle and the sign said it was rated for a hundred pounds, and was a hundred feet in length. That would work for what I had in mind.

I found some candles and what looked like a little stove, just like the one my dad had made for me. This one looked much nicer, with a small glass window to use as a lantern and a retractable handle that doubled as a platform to warm things up on.

The last thing I looked for in the store was a backpack, and I went over to the army surplus section again. I picked one that was separated into three sections, and able to carry a good deal. I liked my satchel, but it wasn't big enough. I sure missed Judy and her ability to carry a lot more stuff. I brought my items to the counter.

"Can I help you?" the man behind the counter asked. He was an older gentleman with a large, graying beard that covered a good portion of his chest. His arms were tattooed from the wrist up past his shirtsleeves. His graying hair was pulled back in a ponytail, and he had a rough but kind-looking face. A large handgun was riding his right hip in a worn leather holster.

"Yes. I need some cash. Do you buy silver?" I asked, pulling two coins out of my satchel.

"Sure. What have you got?" The man reached out and I placed the silver in his hand. He looked at the coins, and nodded. "Let me check today's spot price." He went over to what looked like a computer and clicked a small device attached to it. I almost told him, but I kept my mouth shut.

While I waited, I looked at the knives and guns displayed under the glass at the counter. I had never seen so many in one place at one time before. The other men at the counter had moved down, but I noticed they were looking at me and my satchel. They were trying not to be obvious about it, but I could sense their interest.

"Here we go. Looks like you would get fifty-four ninety," he said. He looked at the things I had brought up. "Taking out what you have here, you'd clear thirty bucks," He said.

"Sounds good. Can I get a box of ammo, too?" I said.

The man looked at me for a moment. "Sure. What caliber?" he asked, turning to open a small cabinet behind him.

"45 Colt if you have it," I said.

"Hmm. Let' see. Got some hunting loads, that's about it." He shuffled some boxes. "Wait, got some older stuff back here, hollow-point stuff."

"I'll take the hollow points," I said. I wasn't sure what those were exactly, but they sounded pretty interesting.

"All right, that brings it to twenty bucks to you. You need a bag?" the man asked.

"Nope, I'll just put it in the backpack, thanks," I said as he handed me a bill with a twenty on it.

"All right. If you have any more bullion to sell, you know where to find me." The bearded man went back to the other men and I took my purchases out the door. I wanted to find a place to sit and reflect on what I had seen, and maybe figure out how I was going to get back to Illinois and back to Kim.

I walked down the street, and I was struck by how normal everything seemed. People just lived their lives as if the Trippers had never been here.

That last thought hit me like a ton of bricks and I actually stumbled s little. Was it possible? The more I thought about it, the more the little things made sense. If Trippers had been through here, how did they have power? Who made that paper the old man was reading, and how was it current? How was the man at the pawn shop able to look up information unless the computer was connected to another giving it information. Where did the food come from at the café? I hadn't seen any livestock.

I looked around with the fog lifting from my eyes. The people here weren't worried about Trippers at all. The wall wasn't there to keep the Trippers out of Illinois, saving what was left of humanity.

It was there to keep them *in*.

CHAPTER 5

"Sir, we may have something."

"I thought the drones reported nothing in the vicinity."

"They did, sir, but then we caught something on the infrared moving past the secondary fence."

Captain Vega frowned. He didn't like problems. He liked his mission, had volunteered for it. He'd been here from the beginning, when the wall first went up. He was part of the squad that got the order to stop all refugees from Illinois. Vega was a corporal then, but he knew what needed to be done.

He knew what needed to be done now.

"Let me see," he said. The private brought up the image on the computer. It was a black and white image, and it was from a camera that was pretty far away, but there was no mistaking the human shape as it moved across the road and up and over the fence.

"Definitely not a Tripper," Vega said.

"No, sir. They never could climb like that."

"So we have a runner. When was this captured?"

"Yesterday, sir. We think they may have reached a town by now."

Captain Vega swore. "Dammit. That makes it more complicated."

"Yes, sir."

Vega thought for a minute. "Send out the runner squad. Let them know where we think this person is. Chances are they're walking around in a daze, should be pretty simple to pick them up."

"Yes, sir."

CHAPTER 6

I walked slowly down the street just trying to process what I was seeing with my own eyes. This was how my world was supposed to be. I thought about Illinois and my family and everyone else in there. I needed some answers, and I really wasn't sure where to go to get them.

As I walked, I saw signs for various things, and arrows pointing in different directions. One of them was a picture of a person reading something, so I figured that for the library. It was the best idea I had, so I followed the arrows.

The path took me down a side street, which was lined with large buildings. I could see that several people lived in each one, and I had to search my memory for what they used to be called. Apartments. That was it. Strange name for them. The people in those buildings certainly weren't apart from each other by very much.

As I passed the last building, I started to realize someone was on my trail. The sun was down past the buildings, and the long shadows played through the streets. I used the trees as an excuse to surreptitiously glance behind me. There were two men who were behind me, and when they saw I had seen them, they started to walk faster to close the distance.

I didn't want to pull a gun in this area; too much attention to myself. I hadn't faced two men before in a fight; my experience was Trippers and one on one. I had no idea what I was facing. These men could be highly trained killers, or they could be backwater morons. The range was too great to take a risk on. I decided to find my own ground. I needed someplace narrow, someplace where they couldn't come at me more than one at a time. I did find it ironic that my strategic thinking was for Trippers, but it would work in this situation.

There was a row of garages on the edge of the parking lot in front of the apartments, and between them was a space about eight feet across. It wasn't the most ideal spot, but it would do.

I stepped between the buildings and walked about halfway down. I stopped and took my backpack off. I kept my satchel in case I needed my gun, and I waited with my hand in the satchel. The handle of my Colt felt very reassuring.

The two men came running up to the garage, and stopped suddenly when they saw that I had not run off. They seemed a little put off that I was standing there, and I used the opening to address them.

"Why are you two following me?" I asked.

The man closest to me, the shorter of the two, answered me first. He was a grimy-looking fellow, with his hair pulled back in a ponytail. His eyes were narrow and close-set, giving him a predatory appearance, and they looked first at my hand in the satchel before they looked at me.

"Following you? Hell, no. We just happen to be going in the same direction, that's all," he said, with a small smirk on his face. He looked over his shoulder and his larger companion backed away, disappearing around the corner of the garage.

I decided to play it easy. "Okay, then keep going. I came in here to repack my bag out of the way of the street," I said, giving a plausible reason as to why I was out of the way and standing there with my hand in my bag.

"No problem, man, no problem. Y'all have a good day." He smiled and stepped back, disappearing around the corner.

I waited for a moment, then spent a couple of minutes transferring most of the stuff from my satchel to my backpack. That left just my Colt in the bag, which made it easier to grab if I needed it. I wanted to strap it on, but since I hadn't seen anyone else wearing a weapon, I decided to leave it in the satchel.

I slung my bags back on and went back out the way I came. I reached the edge of the garage and stopped short. In the shadows, I could see the garage had suddenly grown a man-shaped bulge. I stepped back and shook my head.

"I can see your shadow," I said loudly.

Ponytail man re-emerged around the corner. He smiled and put his hands out.

"Okay. You got me." He pointed at the satchel. "You pulled some silver out of that bag. I figure you can pull out some more."

I shook my head. "All out," I said. I gauged the man standing in front of me and figured he shouldn't be too difficult. My worry was his friend, who hadn't shown up. He was a much bigger threat.

Ponytail smirked and tucked his hands in his pockets. "Well, maybe you'll just let me see for myself."

I found that funny. "And if I don't?" I laughed. I could hear his friend trying to sneak up behind me. Anyone who had lived through Tripper waves could walk quieter than that, and it was confirming the hunch I had earlier.

"Well, then we might..."

I didn't wait for his answer. I spun around, drawing my knife from its sheath and lunging it at the big man standing behind me. He actually had one arm raised and ready to strike. The blade stopped just above his Adam's apple, and he froze in place. I grabbed him by the shirt and pushed him against the wall, keeping my knife where it was. A small trickle of crimson started leaking down his neck, and the big man swallowed carefully.

I looked at Ponytail. "You might what? Actually learn to sneak up on someone? Where I come from, making that much noise gets you killed," I said angrily. I released the man and pushed him away from me. "Both of you walk ahead of me," I said.

The two complied, with the big man rubbing his neck. We reached the parking lot and I pointed back the way we had come.

"Get lost that way," I said. "I see you again, I'll figure it's self-defense and kill you both."

Ponytail looked shocked. "Kill us? For trying to roll you? Where the hell are you from?"

I don't know why I said it. I just wanted to get rid of these two. "I'm from Illinois. And I think I killed a Tripper with my blade either yesterday or the day before. I'm not sure." I looked pointedly at the men. "Good luck."

I don't know what I expected, but two grown men screaming and running away wasn't at the top of the list. They moved like the devil himself was about to bite them.

I shrugged and figured they didn't get many out here. I checked my bearings and headed down the street again, searching for the library.

CHAPTER 7

Half an hour later, I was standing at the librarian's desk. I had found the library twenty minutes ago, but I had spent the time just absorbing all the books. I found a western section that had several Louis L'Amour books I hadn't read, and since they were dusty, I just put them in my backpack, figuring no one would miss them.

The librarian, a middle-aged woman of no distinguishing features, was clearly happy that someone had a question for her.

"You wanted to know if there were any books about the wall? Sure we have a few, but I don't know if they will tell you much. The internet would be a better place to look, but our server is down until the tech guy comes in," she said.

I had no clue about the internet, uncooperative servers, or things like tech guys, but the books sounded good. I realized suddenly that she was looking at me.

"Beg pardon?"

"I said, is this for a research paper?"

"Umm. Yeah. Big one," I said. If it got me the information, I was happy to say yes to anything.

The librarian perked up even more. "Tell you what. You go sit over there at that table, and I will bring over the material we have for you to look at. It will be faster than you trying to find it for yourself."

I sat at the table and just marveled at what I was seeing. I went over the things I had seen and watched people do. I had to find the answers. What happened sixteen years ago? What was the Tripp virus and why did they wall up Illinois? I didn't know if I was going to find the answers, but maybe I could get some clarification.

The librarian came over to the table with several books and a number of newspapers. She explained that the newspapers were from sixteen years ago, and there was a lot of information in them, especially about the decision to build the wall. She warned me to be careful with the papers, as they were fragile and hadn't been laminated yet.

I thanked her for her effort and I came up with a plan. I went back to the earliest I could find, and started there. It was fascinating reading, because I was seeing things from a perspective I had never been exposed to. Everyone I had ever met held the belief that they were the ones that were saved, that they were being preserved because the outbreak was the lightest in Illinois. What I was reading here was that Illinois was where the outbreak had started, and when it threatened to run out of control, the powers that be decided to close off the state and keep the infection to one place. They decided to create the illusion that the world had ended. The power was turned off, radio frequencies were jammed, and no planes were allowed to fly over except at night, and all their lights had to be turned off. The new forest was planted and anyone living within fifteen miles of the wall was evacuated to a new home

As I read further, the phrase that stuck out in my mind from my reading was "acceptable losses." One military commander was quoted as saying that there were eleven million people in Illinois, while there were three hundred million people in the country. That amounted to less than three percent of the population, which was an acceptable loss in terms of warfare.

I read some more articles, and saw that the decision had been controversial. There was one editorial blasting the decision as murder of American citizens, while another article spoke of the "greater good."

I read how they built the wall, flying in sections as soon as they could be made. Concrete companies worked overtime to get the pieces assembled, and the military flew them in. Once the wall was built, the rest of the world heaved a sigh of relief. There were the usual cries of foul, but they were quieted in the guise of the sake of humanity.

As I explored further, I noticed the tone of the articles getting darker. There was no more talk of hoping for survivors, but rather people getting what they deserved. Chicago had been a rotten hellhole for years, with a murder rate higher than most third-world dictatorships. Who cared what happened there?

It was then I saw the article on the Route 41 massacre. Forty-seven men, women, and children had made it over the wall. They were running from the nightmare when the military caught them. Rather than run the risk of more people trying to escape, the army killed them all. That was when they began the patrols of the wall, and they built the secondary fence.

At the ten-year mark, there was some articles that wondered about survivors, and whether or not the Tripp Virus was still active. A little further reading revealed that the uncovered plan of the government was to go in at the twenty-year mark and see if there was a state to be reclaimed. I wondered if any survivors left at that point would be removed as well.

As I closed up the articles and books, I was struck dumb by the enormity of what I had read, and what it meant for the people inside the wall. We didn't have to live in fear anymore; we could get out. We could...

My thoughts died when I realized that there were forty-seven people resting in a mass grave who might have believed the same thing, right before their own government killed them.

I brought the materials back to the librarian right before the place was scheduled to close. I smiled and thanked her for her help, and she genuinely beamed to be able to do her job well.

Back outside, I walked for a bit, mostly in a daze. I looked around and saw that I needed to find a place to spend the night. I was exhausted and emotionally drained. I looked back the way I came and saw a bunch of flashing lights. I remembered what my father said about the police cars he used to drive, and figured there was something going on in the center of town. I didn't want to be in town anymore, so I headed north. There was a single road in that direction, so I followed it. I had walked before, so I was used to this. I did have a fleeting desire to ride in a car just once, but I knew that was impossible.

CHAPTER 8

"Did you see anyone who might have seemed strange?" the tall stranger asked the waitress behind the counter.

"Strange in what way?" the waitress said. Her name was Silvia, and she was a little nervous about the four men who had come into the restaurant. They wore different clothing, but they were definitely from the same place. Their military haircuts couldn't have advertised them any more if they had worn signs. The three men who weren't talking were looking out the windows, and checking the streets. They gave off the distinct impression of being a pack of predators.

"Anything out of the ordinary?" Sergeant Townsend asked. He had been in charge of the recovery team for over three years, and in that time, he had run down several refugees from Illinois.

"Not really. There was a guy this morning that paid with a silver coin. That wasn't usual, but it wasn't the first time we had someone pay with that. Heck, we had a man two years ago pay his bill with an old record," the waitress said.

Townsend shook his head. "What can you tell me about the man this morning?"

Silvia shrugged. "He was young, about eighteen or so. Wore a cowboy hat, but it worked on him, not like the wannabes around here who wouldn't know a horse from an outhouse. Big kid, broad shoulders. Carried a satchel."

Townsend nodded. "All right. Thanks. Did you happen to see which way he went?"

"He walked out the door and up the street. No idea where he went from there."

Sergeant Townsend nodded to his men and the four went outside. He looked up and down the street, then addressed the men.

"Baker, you're with me. Houston and Robbins, you head that way. If this guy is like the others, he should be pretty easy to spot," Townsend said.

"Sir, I think this one might be different," Corporal Baker said.

Townsend looked at Baker. He had worked with Baker in the past and knew Baker never said anything unless he had a reason.

"How so?"

"If this one is around eighteen, then he's only known a world with Trippers. He's a survivor, and might be harder to spot than the others," Baker said.

"Noted. Which is why we need to find him fast and get him into custody. The longer he's out here, the more danger he puts the rest of us in," Townsend said. "Let's move."

CHAPTER 9

I reached the outskirts of town, past several car dealerships. I saw many homes out this way, but they were all occupied. I realized this was not going to be like Illinois where I stood a good chance of finding an abandoned house to spend the night it. On the other side of that coin, I could sleep out in the open and know there wasn't any danger because all of the Trippers were on the other side of the very large wall.

I kept walking as the sun fell below the horizon, and the signs of civilization melted away the houses became fields and the streets became gravel roads. I barely noticed the miles behind me as my mind tried to deal with the enormity of what I had seen and what I had read. Everyone who was behind the walls had a chance at survival, at living a normal life, but they were kept as animals, forced to survive in a world with Trippers and without safety.

I didn't know what to do, so I just kept walking. I knew only one thing, and that was to get back over the wall. I needed to get back to Kim, and I needed to tell her about what I had seen and what I had found out. This world was alien to me, and I wanted to go back to mine.

I stepped off the road and headed toward a grove of trees. Experience had taught me that small stands of trees usually meant that a farmhouse used to be there, and it would be a good place shielded from view. The foundation was still there of the farmhouse, and there was a depression in the ground where the cellar used to be. It was a good place to stay out the weather, so I gathered up a few small sticks and built a fire to keep warm. The glow from the flames didn't reach any higher than the ground level, and the tall weeds and trees around took care of any casual glances. I stretched out, and with my head filled with conflicting thoughts, I eventually fell asleep.

CHAPTER 10

"And you didn't think to ask for any ID or anything when you sold him the ammo?" Baker asked the pawn shop owner. They had spent the last couple of hours running around the town, looking for a tall teenager in a cowboy hat. In Indiana, there were more than a few of those bouncing around every small town from Gary to Evansville. In this town alone, there were a couple dozen, and each one had to be interviewed and removed from suspicion.

The bearded owner shrugged. "Didn't get any bad vibes off him. He seemed like any other young man around here. He paid in bullion, which is a hell of a lot more stable than the dollar these days. Least I know I can move silver."

Baker eyed the bearded man who returned his stare casually. The pawn shop owner had lived here his whole life, and had seen a lot of government types in and out, especially over the last fifteen years or so. There was a big ruckus back when the virus first broke out and later when the wall was built, but it had been quiet since then.

Baker shook his head. "This kid needs to be found. Did you see where he went?"

"Nope. When he walked out that door, he turned right. After that, I really didn't care which way he went."

"If he comes back, call me." Corporal Baker handed the owner a small card and went back outside where Sergeant Townsend was talking to a local policeman. They wrapped up their conversation just as Baker approached.

"What have you got?" Townsend asked.

"Kid was there, bought some ammo with some silver and headed out. Also bought some camping supplies. Backpack, paracord, lantern, stuff like that," Baker said. "I gave the owner a little heat for selling the kid ammo, but there was nothing to be done for it now."

"What kind of ammo?" Townsend asked. If they knew what kind of guns they were going up against, they might have a better idea on how to deal with the runner.

".45 Colt. Sounds like the kid may have an old revolver, maybe a rifle stashed somewhere."

Townsend nodded. "All right, fair enough. Police here have a report of two men who claimed they were jumped by a young man matching our description. They said he pulled a knife and told them he was from Illinois and hadn't cleaned his knife after killing a Tripper with it. The pair are a couple of petty criminals here in town and no one really pays much attention to them."

"Wow. So this kid not only beat them at their own game, but nearly took them out for good," Baker said. "Sounds like he's a lot more on the ball than our usual runner, and he's got some skills as well. We may want to reassess capture and focus on neutralization, sir."

Townsend nodded. "Nothing is ever easy anymore. They said they were jumped near a condo community back that way." He paused and pointed east. "So let's get the others in and head that way. I don't want to kill just yet."

The two men went in the direction of the library, while Baker called for the other members of the team to meet them there. Townsend wondered the whole way there why the little son of a bitch went to the library.

Half an hour later, he listened in disbelief as the librarian related in hushed tones the materials she had found for him.

"Such a polite young man. His mother should be proud of the way he turned out. Good looking, boy, too. Break a few hearts before he's settled in, I'm sure. If I was a young lady, he'd turn my eye, that's for sure," the woman gushed.

"Thank you very much. That's very helpful," Townsend said. He didn't bother to read the material; he'd seen it before. He was there when the order came to open fire on the escapees from Illinois back in the day. It was necessary then, and it was necessary now that he find that runner. With the information the kid now had, he was even more dangerous than an outbreak of Trippers.

Outside the team reassembled, with Townsend taking the lead.

"So what we have here is a runner who bothered to figure out what really happened to Illinois. He knows about the Route 41 shooting, and he knows the truth about the wall," Townsend said. "Let me hear scenarios."

Corporal Baker spoke first. "Sir, if he's a survivor, and he knows the truth, then he's got one option. Get as far away from here as he can. My guess is he's going to head east or north as fast as he can."

"Why north?" Townsend asked. He hadn't considered that one before.

"Get to Canada, get out of the country."

Townsend considered that. "Might be. Anyone else?"

Corporal Robbins spoke up. "Sir, I'd bet on east. Runner just wanting to get as far away from the wall as he can. East will take him that way."

Townsend nodded. He was inclined to agree, but he wanted to hear all options. These men had been with him for over a year, and they were hunters, all of them.

Private Houston spoke up. "Sir? I have to agree with Corporal Baker. This one seems different. I've hunted two runners, and they all just seemed to go nuts the minute they saw the world hadn't ended. This one blended in, didn't raise too much attention, and now he's drifted. I'd say if we don't get him within the next forty-eight hours, we'll never get him. He'll blend and the only way we'll know he's alive is when he decides to post himself on the internet. Remember Chicago Joe? That took months to discredit, and that damn fool was from Richmond."

"All right," Townsend said. "Let's get going. Spread out, take the roads. Check all the houses. Baker, get the aviary on the phone and get all the birds in the air. We need eyes up and we need them now."

Baker nodded, reaching for his phone. "We alert local?"

Townsend considered that. "No, we need to keep this to ourselves for the next thirty-six hours. After that, we broadcast. Let's go."

CHAPTER 11

I woke as the sun broke over the horizon, washing the landscape in bright yellow light. I made a small breakfast, and as I ate, I rearranged my backpack and satchel. I slung my gun belt back around my hips and checked the loads in my Colt. I replaced the older ones with the new ones I had bought from the pawn shop. I wasn't going to go to any more towns. I decided I didn't want any part of this civilization. They had turned their backs on us, left us to die behind a wall, lied to us, and made us suffer for survival with Trippers breathing down our necks the whole time.

I tried not to think about the people who had died because of that wall and those lies. My parents, my friends, the list went on and on. The more I thought about it the angrier I got. I wanted to cause damage, hurt in some way, something to pay them all back. I didn't have any idea how, and every scenario I thought of just got myself killed.

I stood up, and arranged the pack and my coat in a more comfortable fashion. I left the satchel on my left side, leaving my right hand free. I didn't know what I was going to face as I made my way north and west, but I really didn't care. I wasn't a child of civilization; I was a child of the apocalypse.

A buzzing sound interfered with my thoughts and through the leaves of the trees overhead I saw two white things zip past. They weren't planes, and they looked like small helicopters that had four rotors each. I was curious enough that I climbed out of my little hole and went to the edge of the trees. I watched the strange flying things soar away, and as they did, they split apart and went in different directions. As I got a side view of the things, I could see a small bulbous protrusion on the bottom of each. I wasn't sure that that was, but I had a suspicion I knew that they might be looking for me.

I looked around my little hidey-hole and figured I may need to think about traveling by night, But I was going to get moving anyway. I figured I could get out of sight when the damn things came near, since it wasn't hard to hear when they were nearby.

As I stepped out, one thought made me smile. If they wanted to hunt me, they were going to earn it. I was going to show them what a survivor could do.

CHAPTER 12

"Report."

"Sir, we've conducted sweep throughout the eastern portion of the state, as much as we figured he was on foot. Every town has been alerted, and so far, the local authorities know to keep a lookout for a man of his description. They aren't asking why, but some of them are starting to wonder and figure out our interest."

"Damn. All right. Well, if we go with an announcement, we'll have trouble for sure. What about those two you picked up earlier?"

"The ones who tried to rob him? They've been dealt with, sir."

Vega didn't ask what that meant and he didn't need to. He knew Townsend was as good as a soldier as he could hope for. He sighed long and hard. For some reason, he felt his years, even though they weren't that many. He looked at Townsend.

"What aren't you telling me, Sergeant?" Vega asked. He kept his nearly black eyes on the taller man, reading him as if he was reading a warrant.

"Sir, there may be some greater trouble from this one. Corporal Baker was of the mind that this one was different, that he was a survivor and we needed to think like one to get a handle on where he might go. I didn't do that, and I think we lost some search time because of it," Townsend said.

Vega nodded. "We've seen some survivors before, this one just happens to be lucky. No cause for alarm."

"Sir, I believe there is, sir."

"What?"

"Sir, this one went to a library and went back to the beginning. He found out why the wall was built and he learned what we did with the refugees. He knows about what the government did, what *we* did. He *knows*, sir," Townsend said.

Vega leaned back against his desk and let the full import of that statement wash over him. He put his head down to try and keep the feeling of dread from overwhelming him, but it came up anyway. Vega turned his eyes to the ceiling and blew out the breath he had been holding.

"Oh my God," Vega said in barely a whisper.

Townsend was a little nervous. He had never seen Vega like this before. Even when the order came to terminate the refugees, Vega never flinched. His gun was firing before anyone else's. He just knew what had to be done. Townsend saw something in Vega that he had never expected to see before. Townsend knew without a doubt that Vega was suddenly very afraid.

"Did the drones find anything?" Vega said suddenly, hopefully.

"No, sir, they've been sweeping the state. This guy either knows what they are for and he is avoiding them, or he has figured out that they have a limited range and is just waiting them out. Like I said, he's a survivor," Townsend said.

"Well, not for long." Vega punched a button on his intercom. "I want all runner squads to report to base within the hour. Send out the alarm. Seal the frontier." Vega released the button and looked back at Townsend.

"With what that boy knows, he needs to be captured or killed before he talks to anyone. God help us if he comes in contact with one of those anti-wall idiots," Vega said.

Townsend saluted and left. He knew what the captain was talking about. When the wall went up, dozens of protest group sprang up, calling the wall fascist and the government murderers and worse. If the survivor managed to make it to one of those groups, and he was living proof that there was life inside the wall, then there would be a shit storm the likes of which no one had ever seen. Townsend had no respect for those people. They sat in their comfortable homes and complained about how bad the world was, but they never faced down a Tripper. They never saw what a family looked like after a horde had swept through and torn them to pieces. They passed judgment on the world without knowing a damn thing. Townsend knew their anger firsthand, because a lot of it had been directed at him and his men.

"Sorry, kid, but I'm not going through that again," Townsend said to himself as he walked towards where his men were waiting. If one of his men had a shot, he was ordered to take it, period.

CHAPTER 13

I stayed off the roads, and I mostly traveled during the night and around the dusk and dawn hours. The only things I came in contact with were farm animals and creeks. I figured I made about eight to ten miles a night in walking. I would have been able to make a lot more time if I got onto a road, but I knew that the roads would be watched, and the more time I spent under the trees, the less likely any of those flying things would be able to see me. I'd seen several of them over the past couple of days; they crisscrossed the sky something fierce during the middle of the day. I didn't hear any at night, so I thought they were hard pressed to see well in the dark. I wished I had my bow with me. I would have liked to see if I could knock one of those things down for a closer look. My handgun could do the job, but I would have to be close.

I discovered that the town I had found was called Hebron, and I only knew that because I saw the sign thanking me for visiting as I looked back. They were pretty nice there, overall, except for those two idiots who thought they could rob me. I wonder what happened to them after I told them I was from Illinois? Guess I'd never know.

I used the night to travel for more than just concealment from flyers. I could also see from the glows in the sky where large concentrations of people were. I didn't want anyone to see me, because I didn't want to get caught. But I also didn't want to meet people on this side of the wall because I was mad at all of them. They let the wall happen. They let the government shut us up and shut us off as if we didn't matter. They didn't say stop when they could have, and I was holding a grudge against them all for that. My mother, my father, my friends. Everyone who had been left behind for no other crime than being in the wrong place at the wrong time. We didn't deserve to be treated that way. We didn't deserve to be left to die.

The one bad thing about trying to go quietly in Indiana was there was a lot of open space. The crops were harvested, leaving huge open spaces of flat land. I walked in the ditches and the banks of creeks, keeping myself as low as possible. During the day, I slept in what abandoned places I could find. If that didn't work, I found that there were a lot of small platforms in the few groves of trees around the area. Every forest I came to had at least two or three. They were a lot more convenient than sleeping on the ground, and several of them were sheltered from the wind and rain.

I had only been discovered once, and that was by a small boy. He saw me get up out of his daddy's barn, and I held my finger to my lips as I passed him by. Since he didn't scream, I wonder if he had seen such a thing before and it wasn't a big deal to him.

This evening, I was still headed north, aiming myself between a very large light on the right and somewhat lesser light on the left. The route I was taking had me following a road for a small amount of time, and I stayed in the ditch to keep out of sight. I ducked a few times as cars passed by, but as I was discovering, people in cars tended not to see anything other than the spot in their headlights when they were driving at night. I got nervous every time a car passed, and I was looking forward to the time when I could get off the road.

I was about to get out of the ditch when I heard a heavy motor sound to the south. I had seen trucks going by so I knew the sound, but this time it seemed different. The truck didn't seem to be in any real hurry to get where it was going, so normally I would decide to slip out of the ditch and into the tall grass on the side of the road. At normal speed, people didn't see me. At slower speeds, I was running a risk, and for some reason, I decided not to head out into the grass but stay where I was. The ditch was deeper at this point and was home to a small creek that had been dry for a time. I leaned back against the bank and the truck was completely hidden from my view.

The truck rolled past, and it was slow in rolling. I heard boots walking along the road and there were bits of conversation that drifted down my way.

"Heard he's a fighter."

"Maybe. I doubt it. Don't matter if he is."

"Anything on your side?"

"Nothing on heat, night vision empty."

That was a new one to me. I had no idea they could see in the dark or were able to see the heat I gave off. I gave a small prayer of thanks to whoever was listening that I had stayed in the ditch. More conversation fell to earth.

"Vega's nuts about this one."

"Don't matter. He's dead like the rest we catch."

"Towns know it?

"Yeah, they got notified earlier today."

"Why are we out here?"

"'Cause we have no rank, dumbass."

I felt like a bucket of cold water had been dumped down my back. It was bad enough they were all against me because I wasn't dead when I was supposed to be, but now they wanted to *make* me dead. I thought about that for a while, and it dawned on me that I represented what they were afraid of. I had survived, and we were proof the government killed its own. No wonder they wanted me dead. They weren't afraid of infection; they were afraid of the truth.

I waited until they were out of hearing, and then I waited a little more. If there was one thing I had learned from dealing with Trippers, it was patience. It was a full fifteen minutes before I left the ditch.

My first thought was to head into the woods and disappear, but then another thought came to me. I would just follow the soldiers. They obviously figured the area they had just been through was clear, so why would they look behind themselves? If I stayed in between the patrols, they would report all is clear, never knowing I was right here all the time. With any luck, I'd be back over the wall in a few days, a week at the most.

I thought about the wall and I thought about Kim. I hoped she was doing okay, and the Tripper horde hadn't chased her all the way back to the houses. She was safe enough behind our walls, but if they knew she was in there, they would never leave. I realized I suddenly had choices. I could get Kim, get the horses to someplace safe, and we could jump the wall anywhere. Knowing what we were in for, we could blend in easier, and no one would ever be the wiser.

I remembered the stories my mother used to teach me about the Underground Railroad, and how the slaves were brought north to freedom. I wondered if Kim and I would be like that, getting people out of Illinois to the states of freedom on the other side. That thought amused me as I walked on, keeping myself heading north. I left the road when it began to angle over to the east, and I wasn't moving in the direction I wanted any more. Once I was past the two cities, I was going to head west, and get closer to the wall. I knew it would be watched closely, so I was going to have to be careful.

If I was caught I was killed, simple as that.

"Who goes there?"

CHAPTER 14

A harsh voice shattered the night calm like a rock through a window. I nearly jumped back into the ditch, but I knew that would trap me.

"Just me, no trouble, no trouble," I said, trying to look down but at the same time I was trying to see who it was that had hailed me.

It was a lone soldier, a young man of around twenty. He was dressed in full battle gear, carrying what looked to be a very serious rifle. He had on a helmet and the helmet had some strange contraption that swung down to cover one of his eyes. That must be what they used for looking in the dark.

He walked up to me, looking me up and down.

"You a local?"

I realized he couldn't see my backpack, as I was facing him directly. He was about six inches shorter than I was, and it seemed like he was irritated that I was taller than him. He kept looking me up and down.

"Yeah, just trying to get home, that's all," I said. "What's going on? How come you're out here? What's with all the trucks and troops?" I asked. I was playing a dangerous game, but it was the only play I had, outside of taking this man down. I wasn't sure that was going to be easy, and I didn't know if there were any others out in the dark.

"Looking for someone, that's all. You see anyone strange walking around?" The soldier looked at me again, like he was trying to remember something.

"Nope, haven't seen anyone, but it's dark," I said. "Should I be worried? Is this person dangerous?"

"That it is. No need to worry, we're here, it's all good." The soldier tried to affect a comforting tone, but he failed miserably.

"What should I look for?" I asked. Inwardly, I groaned. I knew I just made a huge mistake.

"We're looking for a fella about your height, wearing ..." The soldier hesitated and began to bring up his rifle. "Wait a minute ..."

I grabbed the barrel of the rifle and pulled it forward, jerking him off balance, while at the same time I grabbed the main section of the gun, sticking my thumb behind the trigger, keeping it from firing. I slammed the top of the rifle into the soldier's face, knocking his helmet off and causing him to let go of the rifle. He stumbled back and I tossed the rifle away.

"Son of a bitch!" the soldier swore as he wiped off his bloody face and lunged at me, reaching out with both hands to try and grapple with me.

That might work with someone on this side of the wall, but that's a classic Tripper move that we learned how to avoid when we were children. I redirected his right arm to pass me by and I punched him in the side of the neck as he passed. If he had been a Tripper, I'd have killed him with that punch, since I would have done it with a knife in my hand. As it was, I didn't have a need to kill this one yet. That punch took the soldier to the ground, but he was game, I'll give him that. On his hands and knees, he tried to wrap his arms around my legs, and I gave him a knee to the head for his trouble. He fell back and immediately started to roll over to get back up.

I knelt on his shoulders and pinned him to the ground. He wriggled and tried to buck me off, so I took out my Colt and gave him a good rap on the head, quieting his struggles. I used the cord I had to secure his hands and feet, and by the time I was done, he wasn't going to go anywhere without help for a while.

I took his helmet with the weird goggle on it and left the rest. I had no need for the rifle and it would only serve to confuse anyone who might be following me.

Taking off my hat and replacing it with the helmet, I turned on the special goggle and found the landscape was oddly green and bizarrely lit. But I could see in the dark, which just made traveling easier and faster. I moved at mostly at a jog, my final thought being that instead of keeping in between the patrols, I was going to head overland. They were constrained by their equipment and their transportation.

I, on the other hand, had no problem with walking, keeping low, and staying in the shadows. I'd been doing it my whole life.

After about an hour of moving, the eyepiece suddenly went dark. I took off the helmet and realized the batteries were dead. I buried the helmet in what appeared to be a field of cows. I doubted they could track me this far, but I just learned they could see in the dark and could see the heat I gave off. As far as I knew, the helmet was sending off distress signals every ten minutes.

The eastern sky was starting to turn grey, chasing away the purple night. I had to find some place to rest up, and then I was going to head out. Traveling at night was no longer an option. If I wanted to stay hidden, I needed to move during the day. Not ideal, but I needed every advantage I could gain. I had to get to Illinois.

Off in the distance, I saw an outbuilding that looked like it used to belong to some kind of farm, but it was little more than a few sticks with a roof stuck on top. As I got closer, I realized that if it wasn't for the holes in the sides, the wind might actually blow it over as opposed to blowing through. I didn't really care about that; I just needed to keep the rain off my head should it happen.

Inside the place was surprisingly clean, and there were no other occupants to challenge my intrusion. I used my rope to make a bed in the rafters by wrapping it around a couple of the beams. Once it was secure, I tucked my gun into my backpack and carefully stretched out in my hammock. The beams held, and I was comfortably tucked up in the rafters, out of sight of anyone just glancing in to see if there were any intruders. I briefly thought about the soldier I hit earlier, but then sleep took me and I was out. The wind blew underneath me, but it didn't reach the beams, something I was sleepily thankful for.

CHAPTER 15

Sergeant Townsend looked at the soldier in front of him and mentally shook his head. Outwardly, he was calm and reserved. Inside, he was screaming in this soldier's face, wondering how a young man was able to easily overpower a soldier in the United States Army. Easily!

"Tell me again what happened, Private," Townsend said.

"Sir, I came up on a man in the dark. He looked like a local with his barn coat and his hat. Big man, tall, with broad shoulders. When I realized he was the one we were looking for, I went to raise my weapon and that's when he moved. He grabbed my rifle and hit me in the face with it." The private was visibly nervous, but he steadied himself and continued. "I went back, and when I rushed him, he brushed me aside and hit me in the neck."

Corporal Baker, who was listening to the private, grunted. Townsend turned to him.

"What?" he asked, irritably.

Corporal Baker shook his head. "This one is lucky he's alive. That move is a classic defense move. I saw it a dozen times when we were observing the people over the wall. Usually, they have a knife in their other hand, the one that hits them in the neck. Blade severs the spinal cord in the Tripper's neck, puts him down for good. Hell, I bet they teach their kids that move over there."

Townsend shook his head. "He then took you apart and tied you up. Why didn't he take your rifle or kill you?"

The private shook his head. "Not sure, sir."

"Dismissed. You will be reassigned out of the runner groups, Private. You're useless to me now," Townsend said. The private walked off, shamefaced. Townsend looked over at Baker. "Now what, smart ass?"

"Well, sir, we know he didn't go east or south, he's headed north," Baker said. "My guess is he's going for Michigan. Wouldn't make sense for him to try and go up the lake side of

Illinois. I'd say we pull in all runner units, push them north, while laying a picket line along the Indiana-Michigan border."

Townsend shrugged. "May as well. We've been pulling up blanks everywhere so far."

The two men went to tell Captain Vega, and neither of them considered the possibility that the man they were looking for wasn't interested in staying out of Illinois, but was actively trying to get back there.

CHAPTER 16

I woke up from my hammock after what I assumed were a few hours of sleep. The sun was up in the sky, but not too high. I figured it to be around ten o'clock in the morning, and I was ready to move for the day. I had a two-part plan. Get as far north as I could, then cut back toward the wall and get over. They had to have found the soldier I trussed up last night by now, and he surely told them which direction I was going. I just wanted to get past the two large population centers and then I was on my own to get back.

I kept my gun in my backpack, and then as a second thought, I put my hat in there as well. I took my coat and turned it inside out, showing the red plaid liner. I had seen a couple of men wearing similar coats, so that shouldn't make me stand out too much.

I headed out of the small barn and cautiously looked around. There were a couple of houses in the distance, and a small farm road headed north. I took that road and walked along, just enjoying the cool air and sun on my face.

After a mile, I heard a car behind me, and looking back revealed a police car. I knew what those were since my father had been a cop in the previous world. Thinking about him caused a flash of anger that I had to suppress as the blue-and-white vehicle pulled up alongside me. I didn't stop walking, I just kept moving.

The officer rolled the window down and called out to me.

"You miss the bus?" he asked.

I had no idea what he was talking about, but it seemed like a legitimate thing to have missed.

"Yeah, it left without me," I said.

"Well, hop in, I'll get you over to the school. At the rate you're walking, school will be over before you get there." The officer stopped the car and I had a moment of panic. I couldn't run, and I was effectively trapped into the ride.

"All right, thanks," I said. I got into the back seat and the officer drove off. I was secretly thrilled that I was finally getting a ride in a car, and I had a guilty thought that Kim would be jealous that I had done so. But then I realized she probably had been in a car before our world went nuts and wouldn't think there was anything special about it.

"You play football?" the officer asked, looking at me in his rearview mirror. We drove along at a good speed, and I could see the speedometer reading over fifty miles an hour. It was a bit mind-blowing that in an hour I could travel over fifty miles. The speedometer went up to one hundred and forty, and I got a little dizzy thinking about how far I could travel in an hour in one of these.

"No, never liked it," I said.

"Huh. Figured with your shoulders you'd be a terror," he said.

"Yeah, but my mom is scared I'll get hurt," I said.

"There is that. You don't need concussions at your age," the officer said.

We drove north and then we went a little west. On the outskirts of a small town, there was a large building with a series of fences around it and some fields. The officer took his car up a long winding road that ended in a circle in the front of the building. In the space of twenty minutes, I had traveled about fifteen miles, something that would have taken me hours to travel by foot.

I got out, and thanked the officer for the ride. He waved and headed back the way we had come, going off in search of whatever he was looking for. I waited for him to leave, and then I was about to walk around the building when a side door opened and a small woman yelled out to me.

"New student? Come on this way!" She was about four feet tall and nearly as much wide, her small bulk filling the doorway. I felt trapped again, realizing that if I ran she would call the police and then things might get too interesting in my vicinity.

CHAPTER 17

I hoisted my backpack and followed the large woman into a small office in the side of the building. She disappeared behind a door, and then reappeared behind a counter that ran the length of the office. She pulled several papers out of the counter and was arranging them. While I waited, I looked around. The office was larger than I originally thought, with several women sitting at small desks separated by little walls. I had seen those things before when Trey and I had gone up an office building to hide out from the Trippers. On the walls were several paintings of words, which made no sense to me, and the entire back wall was filled with file cabinets. There were several chairs along the wall, and occupying one of them was a man about my age, with a thin build and lazy eyes. He looked like he didn't have a care in the world, or at least he didn't care about the world. I looked away when he looked at me, but he was offended enough to make a comment.

"What are you looking at?" he asked in a way that didn't leave much room for an answer.

I looked back at him for a second. "Not much," I said honestly, before I looked away.

It took a minute of processing but he decided he had been insulted. He might have let it go but someone in the office snickered and then it seemed he had something to prove. He stood up and was about to move closer when I stepped over to him and snarled right in his face.

"*Don't.*" I put a lot of anger into that snarl and he seemed to get the message loud and clear. His eyes traveled over my shoulders, and it seemed like something changed in his head. He sat back down like it was his idea and proceeded to pretend like I wasn't there.

The big woman who had originally hailed me smiled at me as she sorted the paperwork. I had a feeling that guy wasn't very popular with the office staff.

The next twenty minutes were probably the most uncomfortable of my life. I answered all kinds of questions about my family, where I lived, and so on and so on. I lied about nearly everything, except for the fact that I had parents. Kim turned into my sister, and the horses became my emergency contacts.

After I was finished, the lady made a schedule for me and escorted me to a classroom. She introduced me to the class and the teacher welcomed me, sending me to an empty seat in the back. I nodded at a few of the boys and girls in the room, then stowed my backpack next to my seat. I smiled at a girl sitting next to me, and she smiled back. I took my coat off, and for the next hour, I listened to the teacher tell me all about writing and how a good topic sentence created a sense of expectation for the rest of the essay. I was pretty sure I wasn't going to use this ever in my life, but it was interesting nonetheless. I thought about the books I had read and saw how it applied to authors.

I followed the rest of the class in leaving when the bell rang, and I made my way to the next class on my list. I figured this would be a good place to spend the day, and I had already made up my traveling with my police car ride, so I was actually ahead of where I wanted to be.

The rest of the day went surprisingly easy, and I even bought a lunch at the cafeteria. No one sat with me, but I did notice a lot of people were interested in me. I guess they would be interested in anything new. I was actually enjoying myself, being around people my own age. But these kids had all grown up believing that Illinois was just a bad place on the other side of the wall. They wouldn't accept me if they knew where I was from.

I walked out with the rest of the school at the end of the day and pointed myself west. I figured I had a good day and a half walk ahead of me, and I couldn't count on another police car ride.

"Going someplace?" a voice behind me stopped me and caused me to turn around.

It was the guy from the office, only this time, he wasn't alone. There were two others with him, and both of them were cause for concern. The Big One, he had to be at least six foot three, and easily weighed a good two hundred and forty of solid muscle. Most of it seemed to be in his neck. He was staring at me with small, piggy eyes, frowning with an intensity I would have reserved for someone who farted at a funeral. The Small One was about half my size, but he was different. He practically vibrated with nervous energy, and there was something crazy about his eyes. I had a feeling that he was the more dangerous of the two.

"Just leaving. I don't need any trouble," I said. I swung my backpack around off my shoulder and placed it on the ground. I could see several people starting to form a circle around us, and there were at least a dozen that were holding up small rectangles. I had no idea what they were doing; it actually looked pretty weird.

"You mean, 'not much' trouble?" the speaker asked. He was a sly-faced kind of guy, with mean eyes and a pug nose.

"I suppose," I said with a sigh. I didn't have much hope of getting out of this one without a fight, but maybe I could end the fight before it really began.

"Y'all getting this…?" he asked, and that's when I moved. I swept forward and using my momentum, swung hard from the back, bringing my shoulder forward. I hit him square in the center of his face, snapping his head back and smashing his nose. Blood flew everywhere, and he was unconscious before he hit the ground. He actually fell back and skidded a ways, making it look like I had hit him even harder.

The other two watched their leader drop like a sack of dirt and a collective 'Ooh!' went up from the spectators.

I shook my hand out a little and watched the other two. They exchanged a look and the Big One charged. He ran at me with his arms outstretched, and I knew if he managed to wrap me up, I was in trouble. All he had to do was hold me down while his friend kicked me to death. I waited until he was closer then I grabbed his right arm. I pulled it forward, drawing him off balance. I brought a knee up and drove it into his rib cage. That took the breath out of the big guy, and I pressed the advantage by shoving him away, causing him to stumble and fall. I turned to the little one, and he was already charging, his face drawn back into a hideous mask of battle. I didn't have time to wind up on him, so when he got close, I hit him with an elbow to the head, clobbering him to the ground. I needed him to stay down, so I kicked him in the face, knocking Small One around.

Big One had gotten up and he rolled his shoulders for another charge. I brought my fist back by my ear and held out my other fist. I waited for him to move, and I could see he was thinking about it because he hesitated. Two of his friends were down and this was not at all like they thought it was going to be.

His eyes changed and I knew he was going to charge. He was a lot like a Tripper in that aspect. There was that second of processing when they discovered you that they had to make in their diseased minds before they decided you were an enemy.

"Son of a bitch!" Big One rushed and this time he held his head up. That worked in my favor since I used the opening to slam the fist I had by my ear into the center of his chest. The air came out of him in a coughing bark, and he stopped dead in his tracks. When I hit him, my other hand went back and I brought it forward and up, hitting him on the chin and sending him back to the ground. Both punches occurred in the space of a second, and he was just realizing how bad he had been hit when the second blow came.

That was enough for him. He stayed on the ground while his eyes rolled up in his head. I picked up my backpack and headed out, still thinking the people holding the little rectangles were weird. About fifty yards down the street, I pulled out my hat and put it back on my head, smoothing the brim and pulling low to keep the afternoon sun out of my eyes.

CHAPTER 18

"Sir, you have to see this." Corporal Baker held out his cell phone to Sergeant Townsend.

Townsend saw that the phone was displaying a popular video website. "I don't have time for games, Corporal," Townsend said.

"Sir, I *really* think you need to see this," Baker insisted. He handed the phone over to his superior and then picked up a radio while the sergeant watched the video.

Townsend watched the screen, which looked like an amateur video recording of a high school fight. In it, a lone kid faced off against three assailants. Townsend grunted when he saw the loner sweep forward and take out one of the attackers without so much a word. Townsend knew how fights usually went, and this kid was breaking the rules. Normally, there was a lot of posturing, threatening and such. Not with this kid. He acted like he wanted this done quickly.

"Damn," Townsend said. As he watched, the loner took down the other two. The one-two punch was delivered well, and Townsend went to hand the phone back to Baker when Baker waved him off.

"Watch to the end, sir," Baker said as he went back to the radio.

Townsend shook his head, but he pressed play again. He watched the tall kid walk away, and in the last few seconds, he put a wide-brimmed hat on his head.

"Son of a bitch!" Townsend said. "Where the hell was this taken?"

"Been trying to find out, sir. These kids have really good ways of covering their tracks online. But we'll find him," Baker said.

Townsend looked at the video again. "He's heading west," he said. "Look at the sun. He's heading west."

"Roger that, sir. I've got Houston and Robbins on their way here. We'll get a few more teams to patrol the road. And the drones had been alerted."

"Good. Maybe we finally caught a break," Townsend said.

"Pretty good fighter, huh, sir?"

"Those three had no idea what they were messing with. What the hell was he doing at a school?"

"Not sure, sir. But we'll find out, as soon as figure out where he went. And after that, sir, we'll take him out," Baker said.

Townsend nodded, but when he thought about the video, he had a doubt. The kid was not acting the way he was supposed to, and had beaten them at every turn. Why was he going west? That made no sense. The only thing there was the wall.

"Put out the alert," Townsend said. "He's going to turn north, probably soon. Let's put the teams up near Gary, spread them out, and head them south. I want a one-mile line, nothing gets through, walking south. Check every goddamn hole we come across. Every building, every tree. We check it all."

"And if we find him?" Baker asked.

"Vega wants this over. I've grown to respect this kid, but he's a dead man," Townsend said.

"Yes, sir."

CHAPTER 19

I have to admit, when I woke up in the morning, I felt a little loss at the civilization I was leaving behind. I had walked west until I had reached a sign that said I was entering a military zone and needed to turn back.

I found a place to rest for a while and eat, waiting until nightfall. When it was dark, I passed into the zone and walked until I found one of the abandoned towns. I quickly broke into a house and slept the rest of the night in decent comfort.

Out of curiosity, I explored the house and was stunned to find that the water was still working. I guess that made a certain amount of sense, since they probably figured to come back to these homes once they figured we all were dead. I used the opportunity to take a shower, something I had never done before, but I had read about. The water was pretty cold, but it was an interesting experience.

As I got dressed, I heard a noise and thought I had left the water on in the kitchen. Downstairs everything was okay, so I looked outside. There was nothing going on around me, and I was about to head back upstairs when I looked up.

There were dozens of the flying things, and they were not only flying overhead, they were swooping down and hovering by windows and doors. I realized then that they had a way to communicate what they saw to whoever was controlling them.

Well, that made it a lot more complicated. I had never wished for my bow and arrows more than I did right then. It would have been easy to take them down without anyone knowing where the shots were coming from.

I packed my bags and made sure my Colt was loaded with spare rounds in my pocket in easy reach. I hadn't found what I was looking for when it came to getting over the wall, and I was going to have to be careful with these little spies.

I kept the curtains the way they were and made sure the rooms were not disturbed very much. This house hadn't been inspected yet, and I didn't want to raise any suspicions.

I was in the bedroom, and was putting the last things in my backpack when I looked up towards the window. Staring back at me was one of those flying things. It was about two feet across, with six small propellers keeping it in the air. Underneath the propellers was a small bulb with a dark black spot on it. For some reason, I knew immediately it was a camera.

I don't know what made me do it, but the second I saw that thing, I whipped my Colt out and fired. I hit the thing square and knocked it out of the air. It crashed onto the ground and didn't move. I didn't stick around.

I grabbed what I could and headed outside. I knew where the things were by the noise they made, and I kept going east. I stuck to the brush and trees, figuring they couldn't follow me there. I also kept to the trees, figuring they probably had a couple of those things high up looking for any movement.

I had to keep moving, and I needed to get away from that place immediately. They would be swarming that area in a matter of hours, and the farther away I was, the better.

I could hear a great buzzing sound, and I knew that there was a big congregation of flying machines scouring that area. I kept low and out of sight. Part of me thought to just find a hole until dark, but that would allow too many human hunters to get to this area. As long as I was moving, I had a better chance. The trees seemed to expand into a kind of forest, which I was grateful for. I knew I would be getting to the planted forest soon, but there was a little open ground that I had to cover first. Walking carefully, I almost felt at home in the dense brush.

Thinking about home, I hoped that Kim was okay. She must have gotten back to the homestead, I reassured myself, and was probably figuring out new ways to make loaves of bread into bricks. I'd only been gone for a few days, and Kim knew I could take care of myself. If I were in her place, I'd start to worry after a couple of weeks. Thoughts of Kim caused me to think about other things, and I needed to distract myself otherwise I would get myself caught and killed. I did have to admit to myself that after all this walking, I did miss my horse.

The woods let out near a small pond, and I stayed in the high grass that encircled it. I spooked several deer and a number of rabbits. I imagine the removal of humans in this area had a marked effect on the local animals. I didn't know what I might encounter, but I was careful. I had no idea if wolves or coyotes or what were in this state. For all I knew, there were bears and moose.

On the other side of the pond, there was a larger wooded area, and I got lucky in that there was a road going down the center of it. The trees had grown together overhead, so I was safe from prying eyes. These trees were large and haphazardly tossed all over, showing God's plan for trees as opposed to man's. I figured I had another eight miles to go before I hit the wall. I may get to it by tonight, barring any distractions, like a bullet in the back.

Ahead, I could see the trees thinning out, and there was an opening like a tunnel at the end. I was walking right for it when I detected a faint movement in air. A flying spy dropped down and hovered right in front of the exit. I ducked and dove for the woods, trying to keep out of sight. I don't think it saw me, as I was in the shadows, but I didn't want to take any chances.

The spy started down the road, and in the woods, the noise was loud. It moved quickly, and I stayed behind the tree I was using as cover. I pulled a few fallen branches up and made a small barricade to increase the breakup of my outline. My dad and I had discovered that Trippers reacted to human-shaped outlines more than they did other shapes. Trouble was, it was hard to move when you were covered in branches, so we didn't do it much at all.

As it flew by, I had to resist the temptation to throw my branches on it and disable it. I would rather not leave a trail of broken devices as breadcrumbs to the people hunting me.

I waited until the noise ended, then I waited some more. I amused myself by flipping twigs into a hollow log a few feet away. Probably pissed off a raccoon or opossum sleeping in there, but they never emerged.

I rolled out of my hiding spot, keeping to the side of the road in case the little flyer looked back or decided to come through from the other direction. I needed to get to someplace hidden to spend the night, and I was glad I had made it to the wooded section of the zone. The road continued west, which made walking faster, but as I emerged from the woods, the trees thinned out significantly. There were a number of trees, but they weren't like I had been through before. These lined the road, but the rest were sparse, like the people planting them either were either running out or they got lazy.

With my cover mostly gone, I hurried as best I could. I knew I would attract attention moving faster, but there was nothing for it since I had open ground to cover.

I kept thinking I was hearing things behind me, but every time I looked, there was nothing there. Maybe it was just residual noise from the countryside, maybe it was just in my head. In either case, I kept moving.

I passed under a highway, and suddenly I was surrounded by houses. It was a strange transformation. I passed the highway and there they were. They were all over the place, and they had the trees planted everywhere, too. I kept under the trees to keep from being seen, but as I did, I looked at the houses. They were of a rather small variety, the majority of them being a single story. Some of the two story ones had their second floor knocked off, and the debris just lay in the yard. Among the bricks and boards there were beds, dressers, and some clothing that was still intact.

The sun disappeared, and there was a cold wind coming down from the north. There was a different kind of grey to the clouds, and I knew that there was going to be snow soon. I needed to find a place to ride out the storm, but I wanted to get to the wall as quick as I could. I decided to throw caution to the wind again and move faster than I had been. I cleared the houses and moved through the larger part of town. The sky was darkening quickly, and I knew that it was only a matter of an hour or two and the snow would start to fall. Back in Illinois, this was called Get Your Butt Back Home sky.

I expected more homes to be on the other side of the business section and I wasn't disappointed. These homes were roughly the same as the other ones, but they seemed older, and of different styles. The trees were still all over the place, and in a couple of places, the roads had been ripped up and trees planted there as well.

When the first flakes began to drop, I went over to the first house I could find and made my way inside. The house was mostly empty, save for a few pieces of furniture. There was a nice fireplace that I intended to make use of, but I was going to wait until the snow fell before I started the fire. I wanted the snowfall to break up the smoke and not leave a trace for any idiot to find.

CHAPTER 20

"Sir, you have to see this."

"Christ, what now?"

Captain Vega went over to the monitor of the soldier that had hailed him. The technician pulled up a video from what appeared to be one of the drones. The video was grainy and not in very good resolution, but given what they had to work with, it served its purpose.

The video showed the landscape as the drone passed over it, and then it showed several houses where the drone was looking into windows. The technician stopped the video when the drone was looking directly at a young man who was looking back at the drone.

"What happened to him? Did the drone follow him?" Captain Vega asked. "Why did you stop?"

"Sir, I need to show you this in two ways. First, this is at normal speed." The technician clicked on the play button, and in the video, there appeared to be a small flash near the hip of the young man, and then the screen went dark.

"Whoa. What happened there? Did something hit the drone?" Captain Vega was understandably concerned. The drones were expensive, but they had proven themselves invaluable at finding runners.

"Sir, you could say that, sir. Here it is at half speed." The man clicked the screen a couple times and then clicked play. The screen showed the young man's hand as it went to his hip, and then came up with a gun. It was the gun going off that had created the flash. Even at half speed, it was as if the gun had just appeared in his hand.

"What the hell did I just see? Where did that gun come from?" Captain Vega asked.

"I'll show you sir. I had to bring it down to a quarter speed see everything clearly." The tech clicked the mouse a few more times, then brought up the video again. This time, it took longer to see what was happening, but the video clearly showed the young man's hand sweeping under his coat, coming up with a gun, and firing from the hip.

"Jesus. That's about as fast as I've ever seen a gun get into action," Vega said.

"Yes, sir. From what I have seen, this runner is able to draw, fire, and hit a target in just about a quarter of a second," the technician said.

Captain Vega nodded. "Let the teams know he's armed, and that he's a good shot. Do we know where this took place?"

"We do, sir; the teams have been dispatched already. Should I inform them about his speed, too, sir?"

"They'd never believe it, so why bother? If we said he was a gunfighter, some idiot would want to try him, and we'd have a dead idiot to bury as well as the runner. Better keep that quiet. Do we know what direction he went?" Vega asked.

"Based on the reports from the flying squad, they know he is not north or east. South and west are best guesses as to which is accurate, sir," the tech said.

"All right. Keep looking. And if the drone pilots heard you call them the flying squad, they'll get even with you," Captain Vega said.

"Yes, sir."

CHAPTER 21

The snow came down lightly at first, but then it fell with enthusiasm. The flakes went from light singles to heavy clumps and they stuck to the ground immediately, covering the world in what seemed to be an instant. One minute I looked out and the world was green; the next it was white and not a track to be found. It was funny, but I was suddenly homesick, wanting to be back at my home, with Judy and Missy in their stalls, and Kim coming over to read with me by the fire. I wanted to be back to get my things ready for the move south. I wanted to return home and show Kim I was all right. I wanted to tell her what I had seen and what I had done. I smiled when I imagined her face at the news. I couldn't decide if she was going to be horrified or if she was going to be happy.

I lit my fire in the fireplace, keeping it low. I didn't need the attention from a large fire. I wasn't worried about smoke, just the heat and the possibility of the soldiers using those special goggles to find the house that had heat coming from it.

I made myself a small meal, and tried to figure out what my move was for getting back over the wall. This side of the wall was much harder to scale, since it was maintained and clear. I needed to figure out a way to get my rope over the wall, and to somehow secure it to something on the other side. My mind kept bringing me back to my bow and arrows, and the more I thought about it, the more it made sense. I just needed to make something that would work as a bow, and be able to launch a hook of some kind over the wall.

The obvious questions here were how to build a bow strong enough and what was I going to use as a hook? I remembered seeing some fishhooks when I was younger with my dad, and there was a big one that had three hooks on it. My dad said it was for deep-sea fishing, but the more I thought about it, the more the design appealed to me. I just needed to figure out what I could use for a hook.

I fed the fire a little more and went into the house to see what I could find. I started in the garage, and while there was a number of pieces of wood, there wasn't anything there that I thought would be strong enough to launch a hook and a rope over the wall. I did find some materials for a hook though. The brackets holding up a set of shelves in the garage were good pieces of sturdy metal already shaped into a ninety-degree angle. I took all of the stuff off the shelves and unscrewed the brackets. I took one of the smaller pieces of wood and attached three of the brackets with screws and some twine I found in a drawer. I tested the hook by putting two of the brackets over the garage door rail and hanging on it. It only needed to hold me for about ten minutes, so I was okay with the test.

Down in the basement, I found some white pieces of plastic pipe that looked like it might work out. I chose a piece as tall as myself and brought it upstairs. I needed to shape it a bit, and to do that, I was going to need a little more fire.

Stepping into the living room, I dropped the hook and the pipe and swept my hand toward my gun. Sitting near my fire and looking at my gear was a couple of people I had not seen before.

"Jesus Christ! Don't shoot! Don't shoot! We're sorry! Didn't know you were still here!" The speaker was a young man, probably near my age. He was thin with an angular face and longish hair. His hands were long as well, better suited to doing something refined like building small things than working hard. He was wearing a long dark grey coat and had a backpack at my feet.

The other one was a young woman, probably slightly older. She was wearing a tight leather jacket and carried a backpack as well. Her hair was short, with streaks of purple running through it. Her face was heavy with makeup, especially around the eyes. I couldn't stop thinking of raccoons when I looked at her. She stared back at me hard, like she was trying to decide if she wanted to make a move for my weapon or for one of her own.

"What are you doing here?" I asked, keeping a hand on my gun.

"Same thing you are, looking for freebies," the man said.

"I'm not here to loot," I said. "I'm just getting out of the storm. How did you two find me here?" I asked.

"Smelled your smoke," the girl said. "Watched the chimneys until we saw some mist off yours."

I nodded. I wouldn't make that mistake again. "What did you take out of my bag?" I asked.

"Nothing," the girl said.

"Nothing," the boy said.

"Let's try again. And keep in mind, I don't like to be stolen from," I said. "What did you take out of my bag?"

"You calling me a thief?" the man asked, taking a step forward. The girl snuck a hand under her coat and my gun was out in a flash.

"Yes. I'm calling you a thief. I can see right now my rope is missing, and there's a lamp missing, too. Now we can do this the easy way or the hard way. You choose," I said, trying not to chuckle at the two pairs of really big eyes staring at the muzzle of my Colt.

The missing items came tumbling out of the man's backpack. I kept my eye on the woman; she seemed like she still wanted to try her luck.

"That will do. Now just put them back and you can get on your way." I said, holstering my gun. The man complied and they started for the door. The woman stopped and looked at me.

"Like your hat, by the way," she said.

I took it off. "You got something to trade for it, it's yours." An idea popped into my head, and although I wasn't proud of it, they did try to rob me.

The woman rummaged in her pack for a second, and I kept my hand on my gun. She came up with a small silver necklace. It had a little pendant on it, and when I looked closer, it seemed like the pendant was a coin. The date on the coin was 1941. I didn't recall seeing anything that was from that date, so it must be old. I tossed her the hat.

"Deal," I said, slipping the necklace into my pocket.

She handed the hat to the man and he put it on. He looked at himself in a hall mirror and he must have liked what he saw.

"Very nice," the woman said. The man looked at her and they suddenly were in a big hurry to go out into the storm.

Good riddance, I thought. I didn't expect to see them again. I didn't have enough for them to care about. I was wearing my money belt, so they couldn't have known about my gold and silver coins. I wondered about what they were doing and realized that all these abandoned homes presented an opportunity for those willing to take the risk. I wasn't sure what would happen if they were caught, but I knew it wouldn't be pretty.

CHAPTER 22

I put an extra bit of wood on the fire and worked on bending the plastic pipe I had. I needed to make sure this would work or I was going to spend more time than I wanted looking for materials.

I set the pipe near the fire and let it heat for a minute. I tried to bend it, and it went absolutely nowhere. I left it on for a few more minutes, and when it was hot to touch, I braced it against a wall with a table and pulled it towards myself. I held it in place and when I released it, it kept a small bend. It wasn't much, but it was what I needed. I cut some chord and using my knife I notched the ends of the pipe. Some more chords created a kind of riser.

When I finished, it was quite possibly the worst bow I had ever seen. But I didn't need it for its looks; I just needed it to be able to launch my hook over the wall. I strung the bow with three strands of cord braided together. Pulling the hook back in the bow, I realized I had too much length on the shaft of the hook, so I had to cut off about three inches.

I wanted to test it, but I didn't really feel like going outside, so I settled in for the night. I made sure the doors were locked and my gun was handy.

I must have been a lot more tired than I thought. When I finally woke I was cold, the sun was up, and my fire was out. Time to get moving.

I packed up my things, thinking again about the couple I had met and I briefly wondered what they were up to. After a second, I realized I didn't care and headed out the door. I kept the sun at my back as I went under the trees, keeping to the shadows as much as I could without running into things.

The snow put everything into black and white, and the houses that had color were bright in the morning sun. I kept an eye out for footprints, but I didn't see any. Old habits die hard, even in a world I know doesn't have any Trippers in it.

I heard the buzzing sound and I ducked into a house. I went straight for the garage but I stopped when I realized they could just as easily follow *my* footprints. I went back to the outside and ripped a large branch off a nearby pine tree. I waited for the noise to grow louder, and when I carefully looked out from under the porch I was standing on, I could see a little flying bugger hovering about three feet above the ground, following my tracks. I circled around the house and waited, and sure enough, it started to look in windows. I crept up behind it and used the tree branch to swat it down. The pine needles made short work of the little propellers, and I stomped on the camera underneath before it could see me.

I was running out of time. I had hoped I might buy some with the hat maneuver, but it looks like they might not have bit on that one. I hurried away from the scene of my latest assault and kept heading west.

An hour later, I reached the chain-link fence, and I had to say I felt a sense of relief. For a while there, I was starting to think I was never going to get back, and I would have to stay in this world forever. I'd given that some thought, and in the end, I realized I didn't belong here. I couldn't live day to day terrified that someone would find me out, that I would make a mistake and then it would be over. It was somewhat funny that I preferred the company of Trippers to the people of this side of the wall.

I tossed my hook and bow over the fence and clambered over it as quickly as I could. I grabbed my stuff, and in a little bit found the road. There were a lot of tire tracks in the snow, so I figured they were patrolling this area pretty heavily. I had one shot to get this right. I was curious as to why there wasn't anyone driving over the road now, but I wasn't going to argue with a good thing.

If I remembered correctly, there was another small grove of trees, then there was a cleared space and then the wall. I could see a thin grey line at the tree tops in the distance and I knew what I was looking at. With luck, I should be over the wall before the sun was at its zenith.

CHAPTER 23

"Sir, Omega Team reports a kill in the dead zone!"

Captain Vega looked up from his desk full of reports. "Come again?"

"Sir, Omega Team reported a kill in the dead zone. Looks like they got him, sir!" The private was excited. The last couple of days had been hard, as the captain had been very difficult to be around.

"Show me." Vega jumped out of his chair and followed the private over to the control room. He saw a series of screens and could see the view from the helmet cameras of several of Omega Team's members. The cameras were focused on a man lying face down in the snow. A dark stain was spreading across his back as a similar one was streaming out into the snow. A backpack was a little further away, possibly thrown as he fell. A dark, broad-brimmed hat lay near his head.

Captain Vega noticed something in the corner of one of the soldier's views. "What's that over there?" he asked, pointing to the screen.

The private spoke into the microphone. "Sergeant Panner, what's that object, eight o'clock?"

The view shifted and there was a second body on the ground. It was obvious it was a woman, as her hair splayed out on the ground. She had been shot in the back as well, another backpack by her hand.

Captain Vega looked at the images a long time. Something was wrong, but he wasn't sure what it was. Finally, it came to him.

"Check him for weapons. He should have a western-style gun on him somewhere," Vega said. "Pull up that image of the runner shooting that drone."

The private worked for a minute and brought it up. Captain Vega looked at the grainy image and back at the real-time image of the man on the ground. The hat was the same, but the shoulders seemed a little thin for the dead man. No picture of a woman with him, but that meant nothing.

"Sir, Sergeant Panner reports no weapon, sir."

Captain Vega was quiet for a minute. "They killed the wrong man. They just killed a couple of looters. Dammit!" Vega paced for another minute.

"Orders, sir?"

Vega sighed. "This runner is a clever son of a bitch. He bought himself at least three or four hours as we redeploy. All right, keep the drones in the air, look for tracks. The snow will help us. Tell Omega to bury the bodies. They shouldn't have been there anyway; it's a restricted zone."

"Sir! Flying Squad reports another bird down, two miles outside the fence."

"Bring up the images."

The screens shifted and the monitor showed a low flight over the ground, following a single set of footprints. The footprints ended at a house and the drone hovered back, looking in the windows. Suddenly, a mess of branches obscured the view and the screen went blank.

Vega grunted. "Flew into a tree. Tell those idiots to keep the birds above the tree line unless they want to pay for the damn things themselves."

"Yes, sir."

"All units to proceed as previously ordered. Get Townsend on the horn and have his squad chase down these tracks. Obviously, something was there this morning; maybe we'll get lucky."

CHAPTER 24

I wasn't sure what I would feel when I saw the wall again, but I certainly didn't think I would feel a sense of relief. I guess it came from the instinct that I didn't belong here. This wasn't my world. I was born in a world where you had to fight to survive, fight to just live, and I had no place in this land outside the wall.

I set up my rope and my hook, taking care to knot the rope at intervals. I had no illusions about being able to climb a rope as high as the wall was. I was strong but that was a good twenty to thirty feet of vertical to haul my heavy butt up there.

The bow I had made was even uglier in the light of day, but it was what I had. I laid out the rope and fitted the hook arrow to the string. I aimed at what I figured was the appropriate angle and let fly.

The hook flew up and fell short of the top of the wall by about five feet. I retrieved the arrow and tried again with the same result. I grabbed it again and tried different angles, still just falling short.

"Son of a bitch!" I cursed, breaking the silence of the day. I began to wish I had brought a ladder from one of the homes, but I had no time to go back for one now.

I took the hook and threw it at the wall, and surprised myself that I nearly made it to the top. I tried swinging it around with the rope and managed to get it up on top of the wall, but when I pulled it back, it fell off. I pulled it back towards me, and as I did, I realized I needed to think about this.

I looked at the bow and the hook, and realized I may have another way to launch this thing. I stuck the stick end of the arrow into the top of the bow and swung it towards the wall. It sailed up and over and skidded out of sight. The rope swung towards the wall, and I had to scramble to grab it before it slipped out of reach. I pulled the rope back carefully, trying not to tear anything.

I was very disappointed when the hook fell back onto my side of the wall, but I had no problem sending it back over again, now that I knew how to do it. The hook sailed again, this time with the end of the rope wrapped around my wrist. I pulled it back, and this time, it seemed to be stuck. I pulled harder and harder and the hook didn't move.

I wrapped up the rope and brought my things towards the base of the wall. I left my backpack and satchel on the ground, with the end of the rope tied to them. I would haul them up once I was on top.

I began a slow climb up the rope, walking up the wall as I did so. I kept the rope looped around my waist, which would allow me to stop a fall if I needed to.

About halfway up, my hands were starting to hurt from the strain and my biceps were starting to ask my shoulders if they were feeling the same things. I kept moving, just hoping the two didn't decide to quit on me before I reached the top.

I made it to the crest and swung my leg up. I rolled over and lay there for a while, letting the sun massage my arms and shoulders. I looked over at the hook and nearly fell off in surprise. The hook had caught the other edge but it was only holding by about two inches. If I had jostled the rope too much, I could have been dropped and broken my leg, my back, or my neck.

I grabbed the rope and hauled up my gear, being careful not to step too close to the edge. The last thing I needed was to fall over and have to climb it again.

The wind hit me from the West and I looked back over the state as I stood on the wall. I could see the devastated homes, the abandoned cars, the signs of struggle everywhere. But it was home. I could see smoke fires and the streams of grey and black weren't just indications of people surviving; they were signs of life. I looked back over the other side and I didn't see anything. It was just the tops of trees and abandoned buildings. It actually looked more dead than the side of the wall that was supposed to be.

I felt a sudden pain in my neck and I fell back, grabbing at it. My hand came away wet and I looked at my own blood. I felt my wound and it didn't seem more than a serious scratch, so I tied it up with a piece of my shirt. As I wrapped it up, I looked back over the edge of the wall, wondering what had hit me.

Four men were approaching the wall, and they were all pointing rifles at the top. As I looked, they moved their guns towards me and I ducked back behind the edge and scrambled for the other side. I stayed out of sight and ran along the wall. There looked like some growth near the wall about a half mile to the north, so I figured to head that way. I didn't bother with my hook; they'd just shoot it off and drop me down the other side. The rope I grabbed, slashing through the loop that secured it to the hook.

I wasn't going to let that shot go unanswered, either. One inch to the right, and it would have blown a big hole in my neck. I looked over quickly and saw the men standing at the base of the wall. Two of them had their rifles up, but the other two were talking into small boxes. I aimed at the cluster of them and fired off three shots. All four of them ducked and one of them fell to the ground. I stepped back just as they returned fire, sending angry bullets over my head. I didn't know if I'd hit anyone hard, but if even if it was just a graze, the score was even. It was also a message I wanted to send. Unless you see me dead, you'd better watch yourself.

I secured my pack and satchel, and reloaded my gun on the run. I wanted to be away and over to the other side before they decided that they were going to get positions on the wall and send pot shots my way. I wasn't sure exactly where I was, but I'd figure it out soon enough. The simple thing to do was go west until I hit something familiar. If that didn't work, I'd go south until I hit something.

The growth got closer, and it was more like a small group of thin trees, the tallest of which barely cleared the top of the wall. I was going to have some kind of luck with those trees bearing my weight, but I had an idea on how to get down quickly.

A buzzing sound behind me was the only warning I got. I ducked and a large flying machine whipped by. If I had to guess, I'd say that one was trying to knock me off the wall. It came back for another pass and I shot it right in the camera. The heavy bullet knocked it out of the sky and dropped it down on my side of the wall. I had a funny thought of bringing it to Kim to see what she thought about it.

Another machine came at me and I brought my gun to bear. Just as I was about to fire, it suddenly shot towards the sky. I guess they must have decided three of them was enough to lose.

CHAPTER 25

"You okay?" Townsend asked Robbins.

"Yeah, the little bastard burned my calf, but I'll be good," Robbins replied.

"Anyone else hit?" Townsend asked, receiving head shakes in reply. The other two still had their rifles trained on the top of the wall, scanning back and forth.

Townsend went back to the phone. "Captain, he's over the wall. We thought we took him down, but he shot back at us, grazed Robbins. What's that? No, the drones are not going over the wall, besides he shot another one. They're what? Sir, why? He's gone. No, I don't think he will. Sir, say again, sir? Sir, are you serious? No, sir, I understand. Yes, sir, I understand. No, sir, everyone. Yes, sir."

Townsend got off the phone and looked at his men.

"Pay attention. We have our orders." Sergeant Townsend looked at the wall and sighed. "We are going over. We have to find him and kill him. Vega said we have to kill anyone he talks to."

Houston spoke up. "Anyone? Sir, what if he goes to a town of survivors? Do we kill everyone?"

"We have our orders," Townsend said. "Supplies are on the way, then we head to the nearest gate and go through."

Sergeant Townsend looked at the wall. He couldn't help but feel a profound sense of dread. He couldn't explain it if he tried, but he knew beyond a shadow of a doubt that if they crossed that wall, things would never be the same.

CHAPTER 26

I reached the small trees, and without a second thought, I jumped off the wall. I caught the uppermost branch and let the tree swing me towards the second tree. I stretched out an arm and caught the tree with the crook of my elbow. I rode that tree down and hit the ground. I stumbled and fell, tumbling for a bit. My knife handle jammed me in my ribs, and my gun fell halfway out of the holster. I got to my feet and rearranged myself back to the way I was supposed to be. I guess I should have been glad I wasn't a pre-dinner show to some nearby Trippers.

I stood on a road that ended at the wall, while in the other direction it disappeared in the distance. To the north of me was a series of rooftops, and I knew what that meant on this side of the wall. South of me was a large, empty field, and there was nothing in the way of any buildings as far as I could see. I kept to the road, since it was easy traveling, but the open field was an escape route should it become necessary. There were low hills that hid the homes from view, which did me the favor of hiding me from the view of any Trippers wandering around the houses.

I kept moving west, and it was strange how the abandoned buildings and cars were a kind of comfort to me. This was my home, and for all its dangers, I didn't feel as threatened by it as I did over the wall. I did fell a little under-gunned, as I only had my Colt, so I took half of the box of cartridges and put them in my pocket. If I needed a quick reload, I didn't want to worry about reaching around my belt. When I thought about it, it was a bit of a relief not to have to hide my gun anymore.

The landscape changed as I went West, literally swapping sides. The north became open land while the south became a series of buildings. One building in particular caught my attention. It was a tall building, but the roof touched the ground on both sides. From the front, the building looked like a half a circle covered in windows. The sign near the road said "Lansing Municipal Airport," so I guessed what I was looking at was a real airplane hangar. I had seen smaller buildings like that near farms, but they usually held tractors, not airplanes.

As I passed, I saw the hangar was empty, and I wondered where the planes might have gone. If they went over the wall, chances were pretty good they had been shot down or they had been allowed to land and then killed. At this point, I was pretty sure anyone escaping Illinois all those years ago never found a safe place for themselves.

Further down the road, there were some homes that were near the road, and as I passed, the one on the right tossed a couple obstacles in my path. They were two Trippers, and they marched right across the grass and onto my road. I reached back for an arrow and grimaced as my hand grabbed empty air. I didn't want to risk a shot and call Trippers from all over into my area. Since they were moving at about the same speed, I had no choice than to just trust to my feet and run away.

The Trippers stayed with me, even though they fell behind. I could hear their wheezing and hoped that others wouldn't hear the call and join the chase. The road narrowed from four lanes to two, and I had to work my way around a few cars that were parked in the middle of the road.

On the north side, there was a house that had a small, four-foot fence separating it from the road. An arch framed the gate and I had an idea. I opened the gate after making sure the yard was empty and I caught my breath while I waited for my pursuers. They appeared soon enough, and they stumbled down the ditch towards me. I made sure they saw me run into the yard, then I quickly jumped the fence. I crouched down and waited for them to enter, after which I raced around to the gate and closed it after them.

I went back to the road, and when I looked back, they were stuck in the corner, trying to walk through a fence that refused passage. I felt pretty good about that little trick, but the feeling went away as I moved through a much more populated area. There were homes and businesses on both sides, including a red barn once belonging to someone named 'Vandergriends.' I suppose with a handle like that I'd be proud enough to put it on the wall.

I walked slowly, making sure there was no one waiting in between the buildings. Moving slower through areas that might have some Trippers in it sounded like it made no sense, and I was skeptical the first time Kim told it to me, but Trippers were a lot like animals. Their attention focused on quick movement, but slow movement took them longer to figure out what things were. If I had been on Judy, I wouldn't have cared, but since I was on foot, and susceptible to all kinds of hurt, I had to resort to every trick I knew and a few I wasn't so sure about.

The sun let me know that afternoon had arrived, and as it moved lower, I was starting to miss my hat. I briefly wondered if the kid and his girlfriend had survived, but I stopped thinking about them when I realized they were just as eager to see me gone as I was about them.

I passed a bowling alley, and then the road went through a section of forest and field. The forest was on the north and the field was on the south, and the forest was deep. I could see a few deer looking at me through the trees, and a mother doe led her two little ones back into the brush. I was comforted by the deer; their presence let me know there wasn't any Trippers nearby. It was when there was nothing that you had to worry.

There were two houses on the south side of the road, and I briefly considered them for the night, but then I changed my mind. There was nothing there for defense, and I wasn't in the mood to get trapped by Trippers this close to getting home. I still didn't know exactly where I was, but as long as the road kept going west, I knew this was still the right way to go. If I could keep the fields and forests all the way home, I'd be golden.

The road crossed a highway, and I stopped for a second to try and get my bearings. To the north, the road disappeared around the corner and I couldn't see much. To the south, there were a few homes, and one of them actually had a stone fence around it. I took a look at the sun and thought I might want to try my luck at the hospitality of strangers.

The embankment was slippery and I hoped I didn't look as foolish as I felt slipping and sliding down the steep hill. The grass made an attempt at stopping me, and I stumbled the last six feet before the ground leveled out.

I went over to the house and stood by the gate. It was reinforced wood, and the lock was solid. That was a good sign. The stack of firewood piled up against the house was another good sign. The last bit of good news was the flickering light. There was a lamp in there that meant someone had to light it.

I slipped the hammer thong off my Colt and hailed the residence.

"Hello the house!"

It was the custom of the times not to approach the house directly. My dad said it was a throwback to the old days when people lived much further from each other and the law was pretty much too far away from everywhere.

I waited for a few moments, and the light shifted from one room to the next. I walked back from the gate to let them take a look and see that I was alone. Chances were pretty good a weapon was being aimed at me right now and that was expected.

"You alone?" the voice came from the yard, and I knew they had already checked out around the fence to make sure I was by myself. If I wasn't and said I was, I'd have been chased away or shot outright.

"I am. Just looking for a safe place to spend the night," I said.

"Wait there." The voice sounded young, but I couldn't place whether it was male or female.

Another minute and the gate unlocked. I stepped forward and opened it, seeing my host for the first time. He had stepped back and was waiting for me to enter. He had a rifle in his hands and a stern look on his face. He was probably all of thirteen years old, and I wondered if he was alone like I was at his age.

I locked the gate and turned back to the boy. "Just looking for a place to spend the night," I said. "I can camp out here, if you don't mind a fire."

The boy looked me over. He saw my gun and nodded. "No need for that. Come up to the house. You ate supper?" he asked.

"Nope. But I have some to share if you want," I said.

"No need, there's plenty. The couch should do you." The boy led the way into the house, the polite exchange completed. I set up my stuff near the door and went to the table as the boy served up some cold beans and venison. It was the best meal I had had in a few days.

Conversation was limited, as it was considered impolite to ask too many questions about a guest or a host. We talked about Tripper activity, and he told me there was some activity up north, but then there always was. I asked if he had heard about any activity to the west, but he shook his head.

"Nothin' new. Family travelin' through from the north heard 'bout another horde coming up, but I ain't seen nuthin'," he said. "Anything near the wall? I seen you comin' from that direction."

"Just a couple of walkers I left in a yard," I said. I didn't feel the need to say anything about where I had really been or what I had really seen. This boy was doing just fine. The wall he had around his house was solid, and it would take a horde the size of the one around Champaign to breach it.

We chatted about survival skills and traps, and I checked out his rifle while he looked over my Colt. He remarked that I had a nice one, better than the one he had. I asked about it and he scampered off, returning with another Colt single action. This one was blued, and had a longer barrel than mine. It was the same caliber, and I said it was very nice.

He beamed, and said he'd wear it like me if he had any bullets, but it had been a while since he had seen any. I told him I might give him a few on my way out tomorrow. He said he'd have to find something to trade, and we'd talk in the morning.

CHAPTER 27

I slept soundly, waking when the sun made a mosaic on the wall above my head. It was very bright, and held the promise of a cold day. I wouldn't be surprised if I wound up in snow before the then end of the day.

I took a light breakfast, and without saying goodbye, I left ten cartridges on the table. I figured it was fair payment for the dinner and the safe place to sleep. I slipped out to the overpass and climbed the embankment. I didn't see any Tripper activity, and I moved carefully back to the road. If I was very lucky, I would be somewhere closer to my home by the end of the day.

I moved west and right before I reached the edge of the woods that lined the road I heard a hail behind me. The boy stood on his porch and waved in my direction. I waved back and then watched as the boy suddenly fell back, a red spray covering the door behind him.

"Jesus!" I said, ducking and scanning for threats. Out of the east moved four men, and two of them moved towards the house while the other two opened fire in my direction. I jumped into the trees near the road as bullets whipped overhead. I didn't bother to look back or try any return shots. I was a pistol against rifles and four of them at that.

As I ran, I tried to figure out who they were and I could only reach one conclusion. They were the four men who shot at me earlier, which made them military from the other side of the wall. Why they bothered to follow me was a mystery, unless they needed to make sure I never talked to anyone. In which case, they were going to kill anyone I did talk to.

"Mother of God," I said aloud as I ran. I ducked under branches, ran around fences, and generally stuck to the same direction. If I had my bow, I could make a fight of it, but I wasn't going to bring this crew near Kim. I could never forgive myself if something happened to her because I just happened to be near.

As I moved, I took stock of the situation. I had one handgun, a knife, a pack of some supplies, and I was probably ten to fifteen miles from home, maybe more. I had trained killers on my trail, armed with high-powered rifles that they certainly knew how to use and were willing to use.

I couldn't survive a four on one fight, but maybe I could even the odds a little bit with the resources I had. There were several houses on the road, and as I ran past, I swear I saw some movement in them. I began to open the front doors of every house I went by, yelling inside to see if there was anyone to stir up. I was more than willing to use Trippers as ammo bait.

The more houses I opened, the more I began to have an idea form in my head. If I could get these guys a little further north, maybe in a subdivision with a lot of Tripper activity, the infected could do my work for me. Trick was to get them to follow.

I took a minute to rest and watched my back trail. I could see several Trippers stumbling out of the homes I had opened, so hopefully they might delay the soldiers. Ahead of me looked like a town, so I was going to have to be careful about where I moved.

CHAPTER 28

"Little bastard runs pretty well," Corporal Baker remarked casually.

"Can't run forever, Corporal," Sergeant Townsend said. "Our job is to run him down, take out anyone he talks to." Townsend had been the one to shoot the boy at the house, after they had seen their quarry leave the house.

They had crossed the wall at roughly the same place the runner had, using a hidden door. The wall on the outside had a number of doors built into it that were hidden on the inside. The big gates that the insiders could see were just fakes. They weren't gates at all. They could never be opened.

"Contact!" Private Houston said. He was walking point on their team. He pointed down the road where several people were moving in a slow, almost dazed fashion.

"Well, gentlemen, you finally get to meet the locals. Commonly known as Trippers," Townsend said. "Houston, take them out. Headshots only. Nothing else works with them."

Private Houston crouched to give himself a more stable shooting platform, then his silenced AR snapped out three aimed rounds. The Trippers, who were about seventy-five yards away, never knew what hit them. They just realized that their nightmare was over as they woke in another world.

The four men walked up to the dead. There were two men and a woman on the ground. The men were dark skinned, but their eyes were very bloodshot, and the woman had very blotchy skin, with slightly less bloodshot eyes.

"Christ, that's ugly," Private Robbins said. He nudged one of the men with his rifle to make sure he was dead.

Townsend was looking at the houses, and saw that three of them had their doors propped open. He didn't think anything of it, just dismissed it as a bizarre feature of this side of the wall. *Probably looters*, he thought. *They're all just garbage over here.*

"Let's keep moving." Townsend paused to talk into his radio. "Sky pilots say he's still moving west, but it's hard to be sure." The drones were helping track their runner, but in order to keep out of sight, they had to fly at a much higher altitude, which affected their ability to see anything very clearly with their cameras. Also, there were a lot of wind shears at that altitude, which made things iffy at best. Still, it was better than nothing.

"Robbins, forward. Be careful." Sergeant Townsend took his place in the formation and the squad moved out again.

CHAPTER 29

I ran out of woods at the intersection of S. Cottage Grove Avenue and Glenwood-Lansing Road. Neither of those names meant anything to me, but the intersection did. There were lots of homes and residences to the north, so I hatched a kind of plan. It would require a lot of things going right at the same time, so I wasn't sure of its success. I was also going to try not to get shot. That part was at the top of the list.

I moved far enough west until I found what I thought to be a road that led to the center of the subdivision. There were a couple of Trippers walking about and that was just what I needed. They headed my way and I led them deeper into the subdivision. What I wanted was a lot more of them, but of course, I seemed to have picked the one place in Illinois where the damn things had vacated.

I walked past several houses, towing my two new friends, and they tried valiantly to close the distance. One of them, a teenager, wheezed suddenly very loudly, almost like a whistle. I looked back at him and he did it again, stopping in his pursuit to do it. All of a sudden, there were several other whistles like it, and they came from all over.

The hair on the back of my neck suddenly stood up as I recognized what he was doing. I had seen the same thing with animals over the years. He was calling for help. The Trippers were learning to communicate with each other.

I shook off the chill that gave me and decided to run very fast. I didn't want to be in the circle of surrounding Trippers if I could help it. I headed north and then went east, keeping to the center of the road as more and more Trippers came stumbling out of yards and homes. If I had stayed at the pace I was, I'd have been encircled and killed.

As it was, there were two Trippers that managed to get in my way. I briefly thought about using my knife, as it would be quieter, but I wanted the men chasing me to come this way. I had a bigger horde than I had hoped for, and with luck, I could make the two meet and squeak out the other side. With bad luck, I'd be horribly killed in the next ten minutes.

I swept out my gun, and without breaking stride, I shot the nearest one in the face. The shot galvanized the horde that was forming and the other Tripper lunged, reaching for my arm. It came within an inch before I fired. I got a very good look at its bloodshot eyes and torn face as it fell away with a large hole between its eyes. I didn't bother looking back, I just ran across the subdivision, knowing the Trippers would be in as hot pursuit as they could. Thankfully, they hadn't developed running as their new skill.

I ran up east Center Street since it was the only one that went west from where I was. It took me through the heart of the subdivision and I could hear more and more of them coming out of the houses behind me. If this didn't work, I was going to have the longest night of my life.

I needed distance so I ran hard and cut the corner around a small white house. A Tripper was stumbling out of the house and I didn't even think. I punched it in the head, sending it tumbling back into the house. I didn't even take note if it was male or female, old or young. For all I knew, it may not have even been a Tripper. I could just have easily punched out a fellow survivor who just wondered what all the ruckus was on his lawn.

East Center Street dead-ended at South Cottage Grove Road, and I thought about running into the forest at the end of the street. But the trees were thin, and there weren't enough leaves to hide a decent-sized dog, let alone a man my size. I ran south, but that was risky, since the other group of people who wanted to kill me were coming from that direction.

I settled on going halfway up the street, and into a small cottage-like home near the road. It was tucked under a couple of pine trees and a gravel driveway rolled past to a crumbling garage. The cottage door was half a floor above the ground, like the first floor was sunk halfway into the ground. The little porch leading up to the door was unstable at best, so I checked the house out first, then pushed the porch away from the house. It fell away to the side with the only protest of a single nail.

I closed the curtains and waited for the horde to pass. I only hoped none of them saw me come in here. I checked downstairs and didn't find anything of use. I made sure the curtains were closed and the windows were locked. I was actually pretty safe in this house unless the Trippers tried to get in downstairs. If they did, I could kill the ones trying to get in the window and block the rest out with a corpse or two.

After that, if it got bad, I could block the stairs inside and escape out one of the windows. As I waited, I thought about Kim and what she was doing. I wondered if she was okay, and if the horses were okay. I tried to think about how many days I had been gone, and I was actually surprised when I realized I had only been gone for a few days. It certainly had seemed like more.

CHAPTER 30

I heard them before I saw them. There was a concentrated wheezing sound as the horde arrived. It was as if they had dropped out of nowhere. The street was full of them, and they wandered in the general direction they had seen me before. I stayed in the shadows and made sure there were no light sources behind me. Once I saw they were not interested in my hiding place, I lay out on the floor, placed my head on my backpack, and got some rest.

After about a half an hour, I heard the shots. There were a few to begin with, but suddenly there were dozens. The shots faded after a time and then ended altogether. That told me one of two things. Either the Trippers had dealt with my hunter friends, or my hunter friends had dealt with the Tripper horde. Either way, it was a win for me. If the Trippers won, they'd be on their way; if the hunters won, they'd have their ammo supply severely depleted.

I decided not to bother going out at night, staying where I was. I was safe enough, and I'd rather travel when the sun as going up rather than when it was going down. I was still in territory I was unfamiliar with, and I hoped by going south I might find a road that would take me right back to home.

The shots were finished now, and every Tripper in the area was drawn to them, from every direction. I'd have no chance if I was to leave, so I just fell asleep. Whatever was going on out there was going to happen, and I'll see what mess there was in the morning.

I woke once in the night to the sound of footsteps around the little cottage, but I knew better than to investigate. If I stuck my face outside, I ran the risk of getting it bit off. I fell back asleep without thinking about it anymore.

The sun peeked through the windows with the long shadows of the trees making interesting lines across the walls. I ate the last of my supplies and drank the last of my water. I had an extra incentive to get back home, since I didn't think I was going to find much in the way of supplies in these houses. This one had been cleaned out, and the likelihood of the others being the same way was pretty high. My dad had said after things had calmed down the first time and people hadn't figured out how to hunt or grow their own food yet, looting was the only way to get fed.

I settled my gear on, made sure my gun was loaded and secure, and loosened my knife in its sheath. I'd have felt a thousand times better if I had my bow and quiver, but that was too much to ask for.

Outside, the world was crisp and clear, and the sun lit up everything to a brightness that was almost painful. The air was cold, and the small west breeze promised some snow, unless I was smelling something different.

I hopped down to the ground, and left my little sanctuary with a slight pang of regret. It had been a good hidey-hole, one that would be useful to remember if I ever planned on coming back this way, but I could pretty much be sure that I wasn't ever going to be in this neighborhood again.

I stepped away from the trees and onto the road carefully and quietly. I didn't have any other plan than to head south. I moved slowly, taking advantage of the shadows to move away from the subdivision. Funny thing, I was more comfortable walking in this world than in the one on the other side of the wall.

Up ahead, there were bodies lying all over the road, and the first ones I came to were obviously Trippers. They had bullet holes in their chests, and then bullet holes in their heads. The number of bodies increased as I went down the road, and there was one body that was different than the others. This one had been torn apart, with great chunks missing from his chest and abdomen. Blood was all over the pavement, and there was plenty missing from his face as well. I figured this to be one of the soldiers that were after me, but I didn't see his rifle anywhere.

Further down, there was another stream of bodies and another two soldiers' bodies. They didn't do much better than the first one, and the rifles and ammo were missing as well. Brass casings were all over the place, and this seemed to be where the main fight took place. The first guy must have been some sort of scout that was ahead of the others.

Checking around briefly, I saw a small blood trail heading back east, but I wasn't about to go trailing after a wounded soldier who was trying to kill me anyway. If he had made it away from the fight, then the Trippers who were left had taken off after him, which cleared the way for me south.

I gave the east a small wave and moved south. I was anxious to get home and I wanted to be home today.

CHAPTER 31

"Report," Captain Vega said. He was careful to keep his distance. The man in front of him was a filthy, bloody mess. Captain Vega had ordered all medical personnel to stay back until he had managed to talk to him. The drones had reported that the squad had been ambushed and one of them had made it back to the gate. He had pounded on the gate and fired shots in the air until they had let him through. The men had to shoot several Trippers that had been in pursuit, and for them, it had been the first time they had ever seen that particular enemy in their sights.

Private Robbins had been allowed through the wall, but he was being kept away from everyone else. He was bloody, and it looked like he had been bitten on his arms and hands. He had brought the weapons of his fallen comrades, and those had been removed and were being treated.

"We followed the runner into the interior, and silenced a man he had spent the night with. We chased him into a subdivision and there we lost him. When we reached a corner, Private Houston, our lead, had first contact. He put down several and then they were all over him. More came out of the shadows and then Corporal Baker and Sergeant Townsend were killed. I had no choice but to retreat." Private Robbins looked up at Captain Vega.

"You had no choice," Vega said. "And neither do I." Captain Vega drew his sidearm and fired a single shot into the head of Private Robbins. The dead man toppled over and lay bleeding in the grass.

Vega addressed the men behind him. "He had been bitten, and was dead anyway. I did him a favor." Captain Vega holstered his sidearm. "Obviously, we need more men to solve this problem; it's bigger than a single squad. Lieutenant Campbell!"

Campbell stepped forward. He was a small man, with blond hair and what other men had described as 'mean' eyes. They were just small and dark.

"Sir!" The dead man at his feet bothered him not a bit. He had read all the reports on the Tripp virus and the Trippers that had come from it. He was fully prepared to go into Illinois and wipe out the state if he was ordered to do so.

Vega knew this, and knew he was the right man for the job. "Gather up Sergeants Bell and Stafford. Have them bring their squads to this gate, and get fully outfitted. They're going in, first thing in the morning."

"Same orders, sir?" Campbell asked.

"Same orders. Kill anything you see." Captain Vega was furious. This was getting out of hand, and the more presence he had here at the wall, the more likely someone would start asking questions and causing problems. Vega hated problems.

CHAPTER 32

One intersection later, the road turned into a forest drive. The brush and the trees were pushing their way onto the road, making it easy to stay in shadows. I moved quickly but quietly, taking note of the birds and squirrels that were active. That told me the Trippers hadn't come this way and it was still safe to move.

An hour's worth of walking and I was back in the country. There were no subdivisions that I could see, and the trees had thinned out a bit. I could see the grey clouds to the west getting closer, and I had my doubts I would be able to get home before snowfall.

Another intersection was coming up, and I had to pull branches away from the sign to see what it was. My heart jumped a bit when I saw that it read East Sauk Trail! This road would take me practically to my backyard! I made the corner and headed west, feeling pretty confident in myself. I'd been to the other side of the Wall and survived, and managed to make my way through some strange places on the way back with little in the way of supplies. Although I had to admit, I would have been very grateful to have been riding Judy at this point. I was used to walking, but this was pushing it.

After passing a couple of houses with open garages, I slapped myself on the head for my stupidity. All I needed to do was find a working bike and I'd be on my way.

I checked three houses and found a possible in the last one. It was a bike similar to the one I had back at my house, but the tires needed to be filled. I had to check another four garages until I finally found a working bike pump. Ten minutes later, I was on the road, moving a better clip than I had originally thought. I stayed on the sides of the road, keeping to the trees and brush. The shadows were still my best friend and the patterns would keep any curious Trippers from being able to focus clearly on what was passing by. Since there were few people on bikes these days, it might actually take them a minute to figure out if I was a danger or food, and by the time they got it right, I'd be gone.

I rode down the road, and it was a fairly easy ride. The road was a four-lane highway, and the most interesting thing I had seen so far was a sign with a woman on it advertising dances for ten dollars. At the bottom it said 'All of the Liquor and None of the Clothes.' That made no sense to me at all. Why would there be no clothes, and why would anyone pay for something they could do in their own home for free? I'd have to remember to ask Kim about that one.

The landscape went by, and it didn't change all that much. There were buildings that were falling down, and others that looked like they were war zones. Some had that particular look, like someone had tried to make it into a kind of fortress. There were the barricades in front, the fences and the overgrown gardens. The bits and pieces of life left behind, and the inevitable escape hole. The lesson they learned later, if they survived to learn it, was fences needed to be solid, stone or metal. Trippers tore down anything else. Not that they were super strong; they were just determined.

I rode down the street, passing a small town that had no name that meant anything anymore. It looked liked most of the towns in this area, just empty buildings, empty cars, and empty houses. I wondered what happened to all the people who lived here, and when I thought it through to the end, it was the same story. They were Trippers, dead, or trying to find some semblance of life someplace else.

The road went into a forested area, and it was tricky to get through with the bike because of all the fallen branches and leaves hiding more fallen branches. I moved a lot slower in this area than I hoped for, and the sky got decidedly darker before I made it to the end of the forest. I thought I saw a few flakes come down, but they must have been just the ones that jumped off early.

The next town I reached was a mess, and I actually had to shoot three Trippers that tried to cut me off from my route. I didn't know I could hit anything while riding a bike, but I actually did pretty well. Those .45 Colt hollow points did a number on Tripper heads. If you hit them in the right spot, they pretty much exploded.

I crossed I-57, and that's when the snow started to come down. I didn't mind because the highway told me how close I was to home. I had about four miles to go, and then I would actually sleep in my own bed. I was tired from moving all day, I was thirsty and hungry, and I just wanted to be in a safe place without anyone trying to kill me.

The miles dragged on, and the snow came down in huge flakes now, covering the area in white almost instantaneously. I slid a few times, which convinced me to ditch riding the bike. I had about a mile to go, so I just decided to walk it. There was no Tripper activity that I could see, and if they were out, they couldn't see me anyway.

I walked down the road that went behind my house and through the snow I could smell a fire and it quickened my pace. I went into the back area and approached the fence. I thought I should announce myself but it was my own house. No one should actually be home. The fire I had smelled was coming from Kim's place. Mine was cold and dark.

I went in through the back gate and secured it behind me. I turned around and ran fill tilt into a wall of fur. Judy bumped me with her nose hard enough to knock me backwards, and I had no other response than to throw my arms around her neck. Her being there meant Kim had made it back. She seemed to understand and let me hold on to her for a few minutes. I rubbed the snow off my face and led her back towards the stalls. Missy was there and she stamped out a greeting at me, bumping me with her nose and retreating behind Judy. She was still the filly.

I went into my house and everything was just as I had left it. I was never so happy to see some place in my life. I ran my hand over my bow and my rifle, both of which were laying on my kitchen table. Kim must have placed them here when she had returned.

I took a long drink from my water jug, and then ate a hunk of bread and cheese. It wasn't the freshest meal I had eaten, but it tasted nearly the best.

I built a small fire in the fireplace and set out my blankets in front of it. The darkness crept into the house and put me to sleep. It was the soundest I had slept in days.

CHAPTER 33

I woke to the sound of voices. The house was very cold, but it was warm under my blankets and I wasn't in any itching hurry to go anywhere. I was home, my horses were safe, and the big bad world was left behind the wall.

Thoughts about the wall started to drive sleep from my mind, but the voices outside seemed to become louder, like they were getting closer.

I groaned inwardly and outwardly, and roused myself from my sleep. I pumped up some very cold water which woke me up fully, and then I restarted the fire in the fireplace. A quick look at my wood supply told me I'd have to go scrounging up some more if I wanted to keep warm in the winter.

The door to the garage opened, and I stood by the table with a casual hand on my rifle. My Colt was hanging from the back of a chair, but it was too far away to be useful. The rifle was already on the table and pointed in the right direction.

Kim walked through the door, and when she saw me, she stopped dead. Her hand flew up to her mouth and tears filled her eyes. I had to admit, she was the best-looking thing I had seen in a week.

"Hey. Miss me?" I asked casually.

Kim flew across the kitchen knocking over a chair in the process. She jumped into my arms and gave me a huge hug, burying her face in my shoulder. I hugged her back, breathing her in, suddenly realizing how much I had actually missed her as well.

She pulled back and smiled, with tears streaming down her face.

"I thought you were gone. When you didn't come back, I thought you were gone," Kim said quietly. "What happened to you?" She didn't wait for an answer, she just hugged me again, and when she finished with that, she took my face in her hands and stared into my eyes for a very long time. When she figured out that I was actually back and not dead, she gave me a very long, lingering kiss. It was the sweetest thing anyone had ever done for me.

"Well, hello. Sorry to interrupt," a strange voice came from across the kitchen and I pulled Kim aside, bringing up my rifle to bear on a man I had seen before.

"Whoa! Sorry! I'll wait outside." The man was blond with blue eyes, and a smile I remembered.

"No, you won't," I said. "You move and I'll shoot you."

"What? What did I do? You don't even know me!" the man said, backing up with his hands in the air.

Kim pulled at my arm, but she may as well have been pulling at a tree branch for all I moved.

"Josh, what are you doing? This is…" Kim started to say.

"Kevin. We've met," I said. "You were too interested in my horse the last time we met. I could have shot you then."

Kevin's eyes narrowed and then they widened. "Oh my God! I remember now! I was out by Joliet and trying to get by some Trippers when I saw your horse! You scared the crap out of me!"

"You almost made a very serious second mistake when you reached for your gun," I said, remembering more details. "Another inch and I'd have killed you."

Kevin laughed. "I remember. You had you hand on your gun and your face changed. You were ready to pull your weapon."

Kim watched the exchange with growing eyes. She looked at Kevin with what had to be open hostility.

"You tried to steal Judy? Josh could have been killed!" Kim eyed the bow and arrows on the table as if contemplating turning Kevin into an archery target.

"It's all right," I said. "It's over and done with. But you were leaving, yes?" I asked, not really asking.

Kevin got the message. "I'm just looking to spend the winter and then I'm heading for warmer weather."

"There's a house with a good fence around it across the creek on the other side of the house across the street," I said. "You should be able to survive the winter there."

Kevin looked at me and at Kim. I got the idea that he had thought to spend the winter in another place, but Kim would never forget the attempt to steal Judy. Kim considered those horses her children.

"Across the creek?" he asked.

"There's bigger houses if you cross the tracks, if you want," I said. "You'll be fine in either, and when the spring comes, you can head out without a problem."

Kevin nodded. "I'll get my things. They're in the barn."

I don't know why, but I was grateful he didn't say Kim's house.

"Good luck," I said.

Kevin left and I went to the window to make sure he went out and didn't try to take one of the horses with him. When he had gone and had locked the gate behind him, I turned back to Kim.

"It's good to see you, Kim," I said.

Kim came back over to me and fell into my arms again. It was good to feel her there and I kissed the top of her head.

She looked up at me and asked a very complicated question.

"Where the hell have you been?"

I didn't know where to start with that question so I decided to go back to when the trouble all began. But I needed to be sitting to do it.

"Let's get the fire going a little better and get something to eat. I'm somewhat famished," I said. "Then I have a very interesting tale to tell."

We stoked the fire and Kim went back to her house to get a loaf of bread. She had been experimenting with sourdough bread, and I had to say the latest version was pretty good. Added with some canned apples and venison jerky, I was eating well.

"Well, where to begin?" I asked, as I settled in my big reading chair. Kim sat in my lap, nibbling on a piece of jerky.

"What happened after you got chased off the race track?" Kim asked.

"I ran east, hoping I could lose them, but they never stopped coming. I finally wound up climbing a tree and getting on top of the wall," I said.

"The wall! Oh my god. Where did you go from there? Did you go north or south?" she asked.

I took a deep breath. "Actually, I went east."

Kim frowned. "East? How'd you manage that?"

"The Trippers slammed into the tree and the branch knocked me off the wall," I said. "I fell off the wall and found myself on the other side."

Kim stopped eating and stared at me.

"You went over the wall?" she whispered.

"I did," I said.

"And you made it back. Oh my God," Kim said. "What was it like?"

"Well, there lies a strange tale," I said. I took a deep breath and began my story.

CHAPTER 34

It took over an hour to explain where I was and what I had seen. Kim said nothing at first, but as the tale unfolded, she started to shake her head more and more. Finally, she stood up and started to pace.

"So they lied to us. They shut us in here to die," she said.

"Basically," I said. "But it gets worse." I explained to her about the library and the newspapers I had seen. I told her about the manhunt and the attempts to kill me.

"I don't get it. Why would they want you dead? What harm are you now to them?" Kim asked.

"I know the truth. Think about it. If I went around and told everyone that the other side of the wall is safe, there would be a mass run for the border. Some of us might actually survive the army purges, and we'd tell our tale to the people who might listen on the outside. They shut in their own people and let them die horrible deaths at the hands of infected hordes. People responsible for that would likely go to jail," I said. "Easier to just kill me and anyone that I come in contact with. Who will care who dies on this side of the wall over there? According to what I read, we deserved what we got."

"How did you manage to survive?" Kim asked. "They had all this equipment and you still beat them."

"The people they used to see weren't survivors. They were just runners. I had a lot of luck, but they weren't ready for someone like me," I said.

"And now they're coming for you," Kim said, looking worried.

"Don't think so, but I'll be extra careful none the less," I said. "In the spring, we're heading south, and when we reach the southern community, we'll at least have the numbers on our side." I hadn't given up the thought of going south and picking up that law enforcement position. I had seen a lot, more than anyone in the state, but I knew how dangerous it was over there.

Kim was quiet, and I knew what she was thinking.

"They'd kill us, Kim. We can't go over," I said gently.

Kim smiled at me. "Stop doing that. I know. But I want you to think about something. You know what it's like over there. Why not keep that in mind as a back-up plan, in case things don't work out here? I remember how things used to be, and we can talk to some older people who might remember the tricks to survive in the real world."

I thought about it. It was a nice thought to believe that we could always just go over the wall and there were things we could see and do. We could always find a farm somewhere and just live out our days in peace. Of course, we could do that here, and not have to worry about being discovered.

"We'll see. Right now, we have to get through the winter, get ourselves set to head south at the first break in the season," I said.

"You know, I'm not going to sleep for days, now that I know this," Kim said.

"I didn't either," I said. "Then I realized they were going to try and kill me, and for some reason, I slept like a baby."

"You're a lunatic."

CHAPTER 35

We still had the problem of a wagon to move things south, and I wasn't about to go back to the racetrack to see if we could scrounge another one. The only other place I had seen that could handle horses was on the road to Manhattan.

I told Kim about the horse barn and she agreed it was worth a look. I figured to head out in the morning and take a gander. For today, I just wanted to take it easy, work the trap lines, and stay out of trouble.

Around mid-afternoon, Kim and I were reading at her house after exercising the horses. They loved the snow, and Missy was nuts for the stuff. She kept running in circles, kicking up spray. Every once in a while, her eyes would twitch to the east, and I kept a steady eye on the horizon. Kim caught me looking a few times, and once I stared for so long she brought out my bow to me.

"Not yet," I had said in reply. "But soon."

We were sharing a book, having two copies, and Kim suddenly looked out the window.

"What's that sound?" she asked.

I listened carefully, and I could barely hear it. But it was a high-pitched sound, right on the edge of hearing. It seemed like it was far away, but I knew that would change. The horses and the fence would give us away like a painted sign, and the only saving grace was the people operating those flying things wouldn't know what they were looking for.

The other saving grace was they couldn't fly low, and had to stay high to stay out of sight. That helped us, but it also made me wonder how in the world we would be able to see them coming or ever think we were safe.

But I wasn't going to make it easy, and they were going to find out just what they were chasing. I took my compound bow and a couple of arrows and went outside. The highest place I knew of was the dam, so I went up the road a bit and crossed over where the trees were still thin, even though most of them had lost all of their leaves. I got to the top and stayed near a tree, just listening. The sound was definitely getting closer, and as I checked the sky, I could see a small shape high up in the air. It was a long shot, at the very far edge of the reach of my bow, and I would be fighting gravity the whole way. But I wanted that thing down, so I lined up my shot, pulled the string as far back as the arrow would reach, and let fly.

The arrow was a blur in the sky, and suddenly there was a small flash. Out of the sky, an object came tumbling down, and it crashed to earth in the field behind the dam. I walked down the hill, trying not to slip as the decline was very steep. I reached the downed machine, and there wasn't much left. The arrow hit the thing in the rear, and that must have been where the power source was because the area was scorched where the arrow went in and where it stuck out. I thought about dragging it back to the house, but when I tried to move it, the propellers stuck on the grass and it was big enough to be awkward. I left it alone, figuring Kim could come out on her own and see it for herself.

I made my way over to the dam just as three Trippers stumbled out of the woods. They were very rough looking, and they all saw me at the same time. I brought up my bow and put one down, and then another. After that I was out of arrows, so I started up the hill. The Tripper followed me and had just as much trouble as I did. I kept slipping and the more I tried, the more I slipped. I managed to make progress only by walking sideways, but it was very slow going. I could move six feet horizontally but only about a foot vertically.

The Tripper was moving better than I was, because it was on its stomach, climbing with its hands and feet, grasping at grass and roots. I stepped higher, and slipped down on my back, sliding down the hill. Something caught my foot and it spun me around to the point where I slid down the hill upside down. My back found every lump under the snow, and by the time I stopped, it felt like Judy had been dancing enthusiastically on my kidneys. I scrambled to my feet as the Tripper came sliding down after me. It got to its feet better than I did and came towards me.

I slid my knife out of its sheath and waited, making sure my footing was solid. The Tripper came forward, and as he reached out with his left hand, I grabbed it, pulling him towards me as I stabbed him in the throat. The long blade went through his windpipe and into the spinal column behind it. The Tripper fell to the ground, paralyzed but not dead.

I took my knife out and stabbed it into the snow and dirt a couple of times to clean it off, after which I wiped it off on the Tripper's coat. I took the arrows out of the other Trippers and used one to finish off the third. After that, I used the arrows to help me climb the dam. I went back to the house, thinking about what was going on.

Kim met me at the door. "What was it?" she asked.

"Remember those flying spy things I told you about?" I asked. "Well, it was one of those."

Kim shook her head. "What does that mean?"

"Chances are, they may have seen the houses but they don't know what they are looking at. There's dozens of houses with fences around them, so we probably have some time before anyone shows up. And since I shot from a concealed spot, they won't know what brought it down," I said. "But in case there's others, I'm going to need to find another coat. They've seen this one."

Kim nodded. Then she asked me a strange question. "Are you worried, Josh?"

When I thought about it, I realized that maybe I was. The men who were after me were willing to kill, and they had a lot of technology and weaponry to help them. I guess I might have hoped that when the first group was wiped out they would figure it wasn't worth the trouble, but the bird in the sky told me they were still interested in me.

"Maybe a little," I said. "Couple years back, I didn't have much to worry about. Now, there's a lot more in my life. Lot more to worry about. More to care about," I said.

"More to care about?" Kim asked shyly.

"Sure. Having an extra horse around is a big deal," I said.

"Oooh! You!" Kim threw a book at me that bounced off my arm. I laughed and retreated to my chair, Kim following behind. She sat in the other chair, and looked at me.

"We have some planning to do," she said.

"We do?"

"If these men are coming, then we need to show them who they are coming after. This is our world, not theirs, and they're not welcome," Kim said.

I saw where she was going, and I had to smile. Kim just reminded me who I was and more importantly what I was.

I was a survivor, and to the very bad luck of the men coming after me, I was also a hunter.

CHAPTER 36

"What happened?" the drone supervisor asked.

The technician shrugged his shoulders. "Not sure. There seemed to be a power surge and then everything went black."

"What were the last images?"

"Hang on." The technician flipped through a few tabs on his computer. "Here we are. Just some aerials, looking around. Lot of homes with big fences, not sure why those stick out. Here's a house with what looks like a barn and a fence around it. Lots of trees in that area," he said.

"What were the last images?" the supervisor asked again.

"Right here. The camera is looking east and then boom, fade to black." The image on the screen showed a big expanse of land and then it went dark.

"Slow it down; I thought I saw something," the supervisor said.

The two men leaned in close to the screen. In the final second before the screen went dark, there was a something obstructing the camera.

"What is that?" the technician asked.

The supervisor looked, and then he shook his head. "Feather. Your bird got hit by another one. A live one, this time."

"Aw, geez. What is it with the damn birds? That's the fourth one we lost to our foul-feathered friends in six months. Private Jerry over there lost one to a bat, of all things."

"All right. I'll inform Captain Vega. He's going to have to tell his men to sit tight until we get another bird over there," the supervisor said.

"Can't imagine what it's like over there," the private said. "I mean, I can see it, but trying to live while those infected people move around. Creepy."

"It's there and we're here. All you need to care about."

"True."

CHAPTER 37

Kim and I spent the next week trying to accomplish two goals. We wanted to make sure we were ready for an attack by the government soldiers, and we were getting ourselves packed to move when the weather broke for spring. I took Judy down the road towards Manhattan, and we checked out the barns were there used to be horses. I didn't find any wagons, but I did find some really nice tack and saddle that I brought home. It was black leather with silver conchos, and I thought it looked pretty sharp. Judy just eyeballed me like I was nuts, but I was used to that. I did find a good-sized wagon that would serve pretty well. It was eight feet long and about three feet wide. It had small, eight-inch wheels on it, but the wheels were solid rubber, so I didn't have to worry about flat tires or anything. It looked like someone had made this thing out of spare parts, but I didn't care. I tied a hackamore to it and wrapped the other end around my saddle horn. Judy just looked back from time to time, but she was smart enough not to raise a fuss.

Kim packed what she wanted, and when she finished, she remarked how odd it was that when she was a girl, she had helped her mother move. It took a week and two trucks to get everything they owned from one place to another. Now she could take everything and carry it on her back if she had to.

I had a few more items to bring with, hence the wagon. I had other duties to attend to as well. I was reloading as much as I could, and I was practicing with my bows more than I ever had. Kim said I was getting scary with them, and I took that as a compliment. I was practicing more with long-range archery, figuring to keep my foes at as much a distance as I could.

In addition to practicing, I was also scouting. I set up observation posts in the tallest buildings I could find, and kept a watch on the eastern horizon. It wasn't much, only about an hour a day, but I was just looking for movement. Not the men coming; I'd never see them. But I was looking for birds. Sudden flight and following a pattern.

If a few birds flew up from one place, then another closer, that told me something was on the ground moving this way. That's what I was watching for. When I saw it, it was time to move.

It was a very dark day when I saw it. The sky was a kind of dark grey, the kind that made you want to stay inside if you had any sense whatsoever. But then there was me. A small part of me said I was being stupid, that I should just grab Kim and disappear, let the vast state of Illinois swallow me up.

The other part said this was my home, and I didn't start this fight. It also said these men were the reason my parents were dead. That part was a stretch, but it knew how to make an emotional appeal.

The birds came up, and then settled down. They flew up again, and again. That was not Tripper activity. The birds around here were used to the Trippers, treating them the same as any other animal. I marked the place in my mind and headed in that direction.

The roads were dusty with light snow that had fallen in the night, and the temperature was trying to get colder as well. I was glad I had brought my heavier coat and gloves, and the hood over my head was appreciated. I rode my bike, as it was faster than walking, and it was quiet, too. I stuck to the tree-lined streets, trying to keep under cover from another spy in the sky.

I rode as close as I dared, then I put the bike on the side of the road. I made my way into the woods, and waited. From what I had seen before, they would have a man in front, scouting the way, and the rest would be following behind. I initially thought I would just deal with the leader, but I had a better idea when I rode out.

After a couple of weeks on this side of the wall, the men coming after me had to have survived at least one or two encounters with Trippers. Although, when I thought about it, I never heard any shots fired.

I waited patiently, hoping I had chosen the correct road. There was always a chance I had missed the right path. If that was the case, then this was a waste of time. There was also a chance they were getting ready to find a place to spend the night, as the weather looked worse by the minute. The clouds looked close enough to touch, and they swirled in grey and really dark grey, promising a very bad time to whoever they caught outdoors.

I waited for another hour, and decided I must have missed them. I was very cold from standing still, and I had a nice long ride back to the house. I warmed up my hands before heading back to the bike, because they were the coldest thing right now. I shifted my gun belt and started to retrace my steps. A very startled squirrel let me know in no uncertain terms that he did not like being scared like that.

I stepped out of the woods and froze. Two men were examining my bike, looking it over, but not that interested. They were dressed in regular clothing, but wore military style vests. Each of them carried a rifle similar to the ones I had seen on the other side of the wall.

They stopped examining the bike and looked around. They didn't see me at first and started to walk away. Then one of them turned his head and stared right at me.

"Jesus! It's one of them!" he said. He brought up his rifle, and I shot him before he could get a shot off. He fell back and tumbled over the guardrail that my bike had been leaning against.

The other man jerked at the sight of his friend being shot, then he jerked again as my second arrow found him. He stumbled back, but managed to stay on his feet. He got a round off from his rifle, but the bullet went harmlessly into the ground at his feet. I shot again and that put him down for good.

I didn't stop to gather weapons or anything; I just grabbed my bike and took off as fast as I could go. I knew the other men would be swarming that area in seconds, and I didn't want to get caught in any crossfires.

I needed to be on a right angle as soon as I could be, and there was one within fifty yards. I stayed under the trees, but the snow coming down suddenly put my mind at ease for being spied on. I rode hard, trying to get out of the area. I circled north, rode through a small subdivision, and then headed back towards my house. I went through another subdivision, and wound up in the cul-de-sac where Kevin lived. He was outside when I rode up.

"Hey, Josh!" he called.

"Hey, Kevin," I said, getting off the bike.

"Can I borrow your bike? When the snow ends, I want to head down to Manhattan and see if I can't trade some of this stuff for a gallon or two of gasoline," he said excitedly.

"Sure. What do you want the gas for?" I asked.

"I found a generator, and I've spent the last two weeks cleaning it up and making sure everything works. All I need is gas to give it a try," he said.

"Huh. What do you need electricity for?"

"Music, my friend. Music."

"Music?"

"This house has a CD player and the former owner must have really been into music because there's over two thousand CDs in here. Oh, my God. Actual music I didn't have to make myself!" Kevin said. He was practically shaking.

"Well, good luck. Let me know if you succeed. I'd like to hear some music, too. I'm going to head out; I want to get home before it gets worse."

The snow was thick, but it was also blowing, which meant it was going to be no fun when it finally ended.

"All right. Thanks for the bike loan."

"Anytime."

CHAPTER 38

"Well, this is different," Lt. Campbell said. "What was the last thing you heard on his radio?"

Sgt Bell responded. "Last thing he said, sir, was quote Jesus its one of them, unquote."

Lt Campbell. "What does that mean?"

Sgt. Bell shrugged. "Not sure, sir. Can't ask him, and the snow made the birds blind."

Lt. Campbell looked at the sergeant with distaste. He never liked dealing with men who were clearly more competent than he was, and Sergeants Bell and Stafford were easily the better men. But they were trained soldiers and as such knew how the game was played.

"Well, what do you suggest we do now, Sergeant?" Lt. Campbell asked, putting as much disdain in his voice as humanly possible.

"Find some shelter. Start again in the morning. Sir." Sgt. Bell hesitated just long enough to let Lt. Campbell know how he felt about him.

"What about whoever shot these two? What were their names?"

"Private Blue and Private Connor, sir. I guess we see if we can track them, sir."

"Very well. I'll radio headquarters and have their families notified," Campbell said.

"What's the plan for tomorrow, sir?" Bell asked.

"If the storm passes, we follow the tracks in the snow, Sergeant. Dismissed."

Sergeant Bell walked away shaking his head. *Just when you think he's an idiot, he actually says something smart*, he thought.

CHAPTER 39

The snow lasted until the middle of the night, and I used the time to put together all of the things I wished to take with me. I couldn't bring everything that belonged to my parents, so I settled on their wedding rings and a picture they had taken of themselves when they were on some vacation or something. I took my favorite books, which consisted of most of my westerns, and a few others. I had my money book, and that was about it. I brought my reloading gear, my arrows, and my guns.

Kim had a few items of her family to bring, but the majority of her things were like mine. She had her weapons and some clothes, and a couple pieces of jewelry she favored. But there was not a lot there. We had a good amount of room on the cart, so we loaded up with as much traveling supplies as we had. Missy would carry a load as well, but not that heavy.

Kim was over at her house when I got an urgent message. Our message system was nothing more than a string between the houses attached to small bells. I went over to the ringing bell and looked out the window. Kim's house was dark, and I quickly blew out the lamp I was using and looked into the night. Out in the darkness, I could see dozens of figures moving about, circling the homes, testing the fence. They were deep black in contrast to the white snow, and the moonlight doubled the number of them with their shadows.

This horde seemed out of place, as there had been no warning, no nothing. They seemed restless, too, moving faster than a normal horde would. I wasn't worried about our walls they had held out for this long, they would hold out forever as far as I could tell.

I watched them for a while, keeping back from the window. I wasn't in any danger, but if they saw me or suspected I was there, they wouldn't leave and I'd have to spend time killing the lot of them and using up supplies I would need later. When I figured they would not be a problem tonight, I went to bed.

I woke before the sun came up and looked outside. My friends were still there and still moving around. A few of them were standing still, waiting for the next reason to move on. I was wondering what I needed to do to get them to move on, and I was just about to work up some fire arrows when I thought I heard a gunshot. It was hard to hear, but it definitely was a shot. There was another one and then there were several. The last shots were different sounding, so my first thought was another gun in a different caliber had joined the party. With the Trippers around my house, I could imagine they had surrounded another house in the area and whoever was making a stand had help.

I went outside, keeping low and made it over to Kim's house. She was up and she had heard the shots too.

"Who do you think it was?" she asked, slipping her quiver onto her back.

"I don't know. Came from over that way." I pointed north and Kim's eyes got big.

"You don't think it was Kevin, do you?" she asked.

I didn't answer. Suddenly, things became very focused. I thought everything would be okay, and suddenly I knew in my gut that nothing was right.

I looked out the window and watched as the Trippers headed north to see what the ruckus was. Whoever was up in that direction was going to be very busy very soon. The Trippers numbered at least a hundred, and they faded into the woods and houses down past the cul-de-sac.

"We need to go. Now, today," I said. "Those shots were the men who are hunting me. I'll bring the wagon over to the back gate. You get the horses saddled up. Judy will pull the wagon. If you think we need it, we'll bring it. But we have to go now."

Kim didn't argue, thank God, and we got ourselves out in record time. I was hoping to have the time to go through and make sure there was nothing I needed left behind, but there was no time.

Judy looked at me with dark eyes as I hitched her to the wagon. I had added some side poles and tied them to her saddle. The theory was a modified travois, and I'd improve it later. I climbed up on Missy who was stamping to go, and Kim gave me a smile.

I looked back at my home and suddenly I was loathe to leave. I had never run from a fight before and something about being chased out of my own house really galled me. But the smarter part of me realized that while I could damage the men coming after me, they had the superior numbers and firepower. I couldn't risk Kim or my horses, so the better thing to do was go get my own army.

"Let's git," I said.

Kim snorted at me, but she smiled too.

Behind us, there was an odd sound coming through the woods. It was the wheezing of a hundred Tripper throats as they found their prey.

Rifle shots chased our backs as we rode out down Sauk Trail, just a man and a woman and three horses. Nothing to see here, nothing to be suspicious about.

CHAPTER 40

"Who did we lose?"

"Corporal Carver, sir. Dumbass thought he could punch one in the head and that would put it down. Tripper ripped his throat out before we could kill it," Sergeant Stafford said. He was the other NCO on this mission. He was a career soldier, having been in several fights around the globe. He had volunteered for wall duty because he thought it would be a nice way to ease into his retirement. Looking down at the torn body of his corporal, he wasn't so sure now that he had made the right choice.

"What about the occupant of the house?" Lt. Campbell asked, changing the subject.

"He saw us, opened fire. We shot back, took him down, sir. Corporal Snow thinks our shots may have brought the Trippers to us," Stafford said.

"You think?" Campbell scooped up an extra serving of sarcasm and Stafford appropriately flinched. Corporal Snow was going to hear about that one. "How many did we kill?" he asked.

"Eighty-nine, sir."

"Drop in the bucket," Lt. Campbell said, more to himself than the sergeant. "What direction did the Trippers come from?"

"South, sir. The drone didn't report any activity. Likely because it was dark and there's no lights around here at all."

Campbell shook his head. "Spooky, isn't it? I'm surprised that we find anyone alive after all these years. You'd think they all would have shot or hung themselves by now."

"Yes, sir," Stafford said. He was learning that despite his youthful appearance, and his slight build, Lt. Campbell had more steel in him than people suspected.

"Right. Well, the bike led us here, and we killed who was here. He had guns and supplies, and was probably the man we were looking for," Campbell said.

Stafford went over to the body and pulled out his cell phone. He pulled up a picture and compared it to the dead man.

"Sir? Are you sure it's the same man?" Stafford asked. "This one seems smaller than the man in the pictures."

Lt. Campbell came over and looked at the pictures and the dead man.

"Well, the one picture is fuzzy thanks to the window, and the other one is a collection of cell phone pictures with the sun as photo-bomber," he said. "What we have as proof is bike tracks leading away from the scene of a double murder, and ending at this place with this man. I'd say we have the better evidence."

"Stafford, get the men in the house. We'll stay here for the rest of the day and then head back towards Indiana in the morning."

"Sir?"

"Yes?"

"Don't mean to speak out of turn, sir, but Captain Vega killed the last man to come out of Illinois," Stafford said quietly, making sure none of the other men around heard him.

Lt. Campbell thought for a moment. "Point taken, Sergeant. But that man had been bitten by the Trippers. He was a dead man anyway. We've not received so much as a scratch, and there's no blood on any of us. We should be okay. Think of it this way, Sergeant. We've just gone where no one else on earth has been outside these walls. Says something about our careers, hey?"

Stafford wasn't so sure, but he was too good of a soldier to say so. He had a bad feeling about what might happen once they crossed back over the wall, and he had an idea as to what to do about it.

What Stafford and Campbell didn't realize, was their little battle had been heard for miles, and there were hundreds and hundreds of Trippers heading in their direction.

The other thing they didn't know was the Trippers had been evolving, and they were hungry.

CHAPTER 41

"I'll admit it, we should have gotten a sled," I said.

"It's not so bad," Kim said, trying to be helpful.

"The snow is sticking to the tires, and it just isn't working," I said, looking down at the wheels. Judy was pulling pretty well, but I could see she was having some trouble.

"Let's find a place to spend the night, and we'll get the horses taken care of. Then we can go see if we can find something better." I was not so egotistical that I was unwilling to admit when I had made a mistake. I thought the tires would make it through the snow, but they were not meant for that kind of travel.

"What do you think happened back at Kevin's house? Do you think he's okay?" Kim asked. "All those Trippers headed in his direction."

"Don't know. He's a survivor, so he wouldn't pick a place that he couldn't defend. We don't even know he settled in that direction. Chances are, he went further in to be closer to a water source," I said. That's what I would have done.

Kim thought about it. "Good point. He's probably fine, wondering what all the fuss was about last night and this morning." She thought some more. "Do you think the soldiers would hurt him?"

"You seem awfully interested in his health this fine day, Kim. Do you want to head back and check on him? I'll wait with the horses once we find a place." I was being sarcastic, but I was also feeling something that wasn't very comfortable. I don't recall ever being jealous of anything in my life, so this was an unfamiliar sensation.

Kim smiled at me. "Don't be that way. No, I'm where I want to be. I just was curious. Being killed like that boy for no reason other than talking to you isn't right, even for someone who tried to take Judy." Kim leaned over and patted Judy on the neck who responded with a shake of her head.

I felt better, and we moved along at a decent pace. We were south of the homestead, having taken Harlem south past Laraway road and continuing south on it. It led us straight into farm country, and there would likely be some good farms and barns to spend the night in. I knew there were some subdivisions down this way as well, since I had ridden this way with my father several years ago.

About noon, we made it to a small house and barn off the main road. The house was back from the main road about a hundred yards, and behind it was a barn-shaped garage. It was interesting in that it had two garage doors and what looked like a small living area or workshop above the garage.

I pointed it out to Kim who nodded, and we turned our horses up to the house and barn. There wasn't any fence, so I figured it was just another one of those houses that people left behind when they were trying to get to someplace else. Sad truth was that when the world ended in here, every other place was just as safe as the one you left behind. It was what you made it, not anything else.

I checked out the garage and saw through the window that the right side was open. I tried the door, and to my surprise, it opened easily. I opened the garage door and Kim led the horses inside. I used a nearby extension cord to make a kind of stall for them, and Kim helped me push the other car out of the garage. It rolled backwards for a bit then slewed sideways into the bushes. Kim said it would help increase the illusion that this place was abandoned if the car was just tossed aside like that.

I went upstairs and found that it was a workshop, with large woodworking machines. There was a smaller room in the back of the workshop area, and I went in there carefully. It turned out that the back room was a reloading room, much to my delight, but after careful inspection, it seemed that whoever lived here was interested in only reloading rifle ammunition. There was a safe, but it was empty of guns. In another cabinet, under a pile of books, was a box of 30-06 ammunition and a box of .308 Winchester ammunition. I happily took the .308, as I still had that rifle. I was gratified to be able to shoot back at long range if someone was trying that game on me. I had tried the rifle before and its range was impressive.

A quick look out the window showed a long yard and there was a pond at the back end of it. That solved my water for my horse's problem. The other problem I had was putting it in something. There were not troughs here, so we'd have to find something.

Kim was waiting for me downstairs, and together we went over to the house. I told Kim about the pond, and she said she saw some buckets in the garage so that problem was solved.

The house was locked in the front, but the back door was unlocked. It was amazing how many homes were like that. We went in and looked around. We didn't talk, just looked around. The house was simple, and furnished that way. There was nothing in the way of food, but that wasn't what I was looking for. The kitchen was a bit dusty but uncluttered. The living room consisted of three chairs and a couch, and a small bookcase of paperbacks. I gave the books the once over, but there was nothing of interest to me there. Kim picked out a couple, shrugging.

I moved toward the other rooms in the house; one looked like an office and the other was a storeroom of sorts. I walked back and the floor creaked under my boot. Kim was standing in front of me and we both heard it at the same time.

The ceiling, directly above me, creaked in response.

I looked at Kim and she shook her head, alternating from looking at me to looking at the ceiling. I stepped back on the creaking board, and the ceiling above me spoke again.

I drew my Colt and carefully walked towards the stairs. As I did, there was another board that creaked and a second creak came from the ceiling in reply, this time closer to where I was. The creaks were definitely following me.

I got to the stairs without another noise and I took the first step up, leading with my Colt in my right hand and my knife in my left, just for good measure.

The stairs turned about halfway up, and when I stepped on the landing, it creaked again. There were two creaks in reply, both of them getting closer. I could see the hallway at the top of the stairs, and it went in both directions. I took another step and decided to lay on the stairs and look both ways. I would still have a retreat if anything was there.

I dropped onto the stairs and looked left and right quickly. There was nothing to my left, but to my right there was a Tripper. She saw me as I saw her and immediately charged. I launched myself backwards and retreated down the steps, spinning around as I got some space. The Tripper was down the stairs almost as fast, and she came at me with a horrendous wheeze in her throat. Her clothes were old and threadbare, and her eyes were deep red. If she wasn't an original Tripper, I had never seen one.

I raised my gun and fired, missing as she tripped over the rug and landed at my feet. She scrambled quickly and got up on all fours, lunging and grabbing my foot. Her teeth bit at my calf, and I fired again, this time at point-blank range at the top of her head. She collapsed in a heap, wheezing her last.

Kim rushed over.

"Did she get you?" She knelt down to check my leg.

I pulled her up. "No, she just bit my boot. I'm okay."

"Your dad's boots?"

"Yep."

Kim nodded. "Then you're good. Let's get her outside and check for any others."

"If there were any others, they'd be here by now," I said.

"That's true. Grab her arms, will you?"

My father left me a pair of boots he had modified when the Trippers came out to play. They were thick leather, and he had placed strips of metal in between the layers. No Tripper could ever bite through them. I ejected the shells I had fired and replaced them from my belt.

CHAPTER 42

We dragged the Tripper outside and buried her in a shallow grave. I stuck a crude cross in the ground and gave it no more thought. It was better than I gave most of the Trippers I killed, but then I never knew where any of them lived. This one died in her home, and it seemed right to bury her here. After that, we gathered some water for the horses and made sure they were secure for the evening. Judy and Pumpkin were tired but Missy had energy for some reason, so I saddled her up again and took her out for a quick run up and down the road. She seemed to love running through the snow and causing large sprays of ice to fly from her hooves.

I was looking for a subdivision, and fortunately, there was one to the south. It consisted of many large houses, so I figured they had to have what we were looking for. It would have been fantastic to find something at the house we chose to stay in for the night, but that kind of luck seemed to be reserved for children and fools. I can't lay claim to the former, but I'd not want to hear anyone's opinion about me concerning the latter.

I brought Missy back, and Kim and I unlimbered our bows and slung our full quivers over our backs. I had my Colt and Kim had a small 9mm handgun she had picked up when I was visiting the rest of the state. It rode in a holster on her hip, slightly forward of her leg.

We trekked south towards the subdivision, noting the time of day. I figured it would take about an hour to find something, and it was about a fifteen-minute walk to the subdivision. Without Tripper interference, I figured we'd need to break into two or three homes, four at the most for what we needed. Before we left the house and horses, I pulled a branch from a tree and swept our tracks away. Anyone who knew how to track wouldn't be fooled for very long, but I didn't feel the need to advertise. Kim reminded me that Judy wasn't one to tolerate other riders, and Missy was a terror when she was riled up, so Judy being nervous would rile her up right quick.

The subdivision was a shorter walk than I thought, I told Kim about some of the places I had seen when I wandered around. I told her about the fight at Fort Du Chartes, and she gasped in the appropriate places.

The first house was a large one, and I wanted to try it, but Kim pointed to the one across the street that looked like it had a playset in the back yard. Where there were kids, there might be what we were looking for.

The area was quiet, and I didn't see any sign of Tripper activity, but that didn't mean there weren't any. I had the strange feeling I was being watched, but I couldn't see where it might be coming from. I thought about a machine in the sky, but I couldn't hear anything. I was carrying the wrong bow for that anyway. I had my recurve, not my compound.

Kim broke open the door to the garage and we went inside. There was one car in there and several kid's toys like bikes and balls and such. Over on the wall, there was a bunch of shelves and there were some sleds. I grabbed the two sleds that were there that looked like big plates. The other two were just large strips of plastic that I didn't think were going to work.

"Well, that's half of it, anyway," I said. "If we could find two more, we'd be in business."

"Let's keep looking. I don't think our luck will repeat itself too soon," Kim replied.

I was of the same mind, so we went back outside and I placed the sleds at the end of the driveway to pick up later when we left. We went to four other houses, and while we didn't find any Trippers, I also couldn't shake the feeling that we were being watched. I looked at the windows of several houses, and tried to see if there was any movement at all, but there was nothing.

When we left the final house in a small circle of them, Kim pointed to the end of the driveway of the first house we had visited.

"Look!"

I followed her line of sight and saw that three more sleds just like the ones we had found were sitting on the edge of the driveway. Just to be safe, I nocked an arrow and Kim did the same. I led the way and saw that there were brush marks in the snow, indicating someone had also wiped out their tracks. They had done a better job than I had, and even I would have trouble tracing them back to where they had come from.

"Josh, look at this." Kim pointed to the driveway of the house we found the sleds in. The snow had been brushed clean of footprints, but there was a message written in the snow:

If these are what you need, take them and go.
Please don't kill us.

I pondered that last statement for a minute. I had the distinct feeling that if I tried to find whoever gave us these and left this note, I'd be dead very quickly. They had managed to figure out what we were looking for, come out and drop the sleds off, write a note, and remove their tracks. All without us even knowing they were here. That told me about a level of survival that even I hadn't reached. Their defense wasn't walls or bullets or arrows. Their defense and possibly their offense was invisibility.

They had done me a favor, so I was doing them one in return. Underneath their note, I wrote one of my own with my arrow.

If you see several men dressed alike, all carrying rifles, do not approach them. They are not from here and they mean to kill you.

Kim looked at my note and then at me. She didn't say anything, she just gathered up two of the sleds and waited for me to get the other three. I put my arrow back in my quiver and hung my bow over my back. I carried the sleds in my left arm and purposefully moved my coat back behind my Colt. I knew they could see me, and I wanted them to know that coming after me was also a losing proposition.

CHAPTER 43

Kim and I made it back to the barn with about three hours of daylight left. While Kim built a fire in the house and got dinner going, I took the opportunity to attach the sleds to the wheels of the wagon. It wasn't anything fancy; it was just bits of rope tying the sled's handles to the wagon. Judy looked at me like I was nuts, but when she pulled that wagon tomorrow, she'll see what was what.

I stepped out of the garage and closed the door. The sun was casting long shadows to the east and in between the house and the barn was a streak of light that turned the snow orange. I admired it for a few minutes, then took up my bow. I stepped into the light, and as I did, I whipped out an arrow and sent it flying towards the road. It had barely left my hand when I was pulling another arrow out and sending it after the first one, only this time slightly to the left.

The arrows hit the ground near the driveway, impacting the snow on either side of a small mound of snow and ice. I put another one on the string as the mound of snow stood up and raised its hands in the air.

I walked halfway down the driveway and holding the arrow at the ready with my left hand, I motioned for the mound to come forward. It walked slowly in my direction, and I could see the mound was little more than a blanket that had been painted to look like snow and ice. If I hadn't walked by that part of the driveway just a few hours ago I wouldn't have noticed it at all. But the setting sun had cast a shadow where there shouldn't have been one.

The mound took the blanket off, and I was a little surprised to see it was a girl. She was young, about my age, and had a wary look about her. Her dark hair was pulled back from her face and she was armed only with a long knife.

"That's far enough. Are you one of the ones who left me the note in the snow?" I asked, easing the string on my bow. I left the arrow where it was and my hand on the string.

The girl stared at me for a moment then nodded once.

"What did you mean by your note?" she asked. Her voice was barely above a whisper.

I told her about the men who were hunting me, and told her about the boy they had killed. I wasn't sure they were still after me, but I didn't want anyone else getting killed for it.

When I finished, the girl thanked me and told me about her community. Instead of running, they had perfected the art of hiding in plain sight. The houses they lived in all had gardens that they planted in the attics, with the roofs opened up to catch the sun and rain. They hunted and scavenged, and if strangers or Trippers came by, they hid. As it turned out, the houses Kim and I went into were actually occupied. We just never saw them. That news actually creeped me out a bit. When she finished, she started back down the way she had come. I called out to her before she left.

"How many of you are there?" I was curious as to how many were surviving like her.

The girl smiled. "Over five hundred. If you come back this way, announce yourself that you knew Grace, and they'll come to meet you." With that, she walked away.

I met Kim as I went inside the door and she was putting away my rifle.

"Do you think there are any of them in here?" she asked.

"Not with the Tripper here. But they sure managed to adapt, didn't they?" I said.

"How did you see her?" Kim asked, pulling the pot off the fire. She had made a small stew.

"The sun. She cast a shadow where there wasn't supposed to be one," I said.

"Nice shooting by the way. You going to get those arrows so we're not advertising we're here?" Kim asked.

"Yes, ma'am," I said, heading for the door.

CHAPTER 44

Captain Vega was reading reports when one of the drone techs came in.

"Sir? Am I bothering you, sir?" he asked.

Vega looked up. "No, what is it?"

"Sir, I have a video on Lt. Campbell's position."

"And?"

"And I think you need to come see it, sir."

Captain Vega sighed. "How bad this time, Private?"

"Sir, you need to see it for yourself, sir"

"That bad?"

"We've learned some new things, sir, and they're pretty disturbing," the private said.

"I'll be right there." Captain Vega waited until the private was gone and then he lay back in his chair and stared at the ceiling. *This is getting annoying. The only man I have left with Tripper experience is me*, he thought. *Maybe that's what I have to do.*

Vega left his office after a few minutes and headed down to the drone drivers' room. He felt like he had spent more time in there the last few days than he had in the past five years.

When he entered, the men in the room stood at attention, but relaxed when he waved a hand at them. They were standing around a screen, and Vega made his way over to it.

"Here you go, sir. It's pretty grim. I couldn't keep the bird around too long; we don't have the air time the other drones do. I'll show you the previous video," the technician/pilot said.

"What am I looking at now?" Vega asked.

"What's left, sir."

It was a scene straight out of hell. Hundreds of Trippers were covering a small area, what looked like the outside of a house. There were several small groups of Trippers crouched on the ground, and Vega realized as he watched that they were feeding on something. With a sick feeling in his stomach, Captain Vega realized that they were eating his men.

"Jesus. What on earth happened?" Vega said. It was one thing to think about what the Trippers had done in the past; it was another to see what they were capable of up close and personal.

"Let me show you, sir. Here's the video we managed to get. It's not great. We had to splice it between two drones; one was coming back while the other was going out." The tech played with the screen for a minute, then the video came up.

Vega watched as the men he had sent out spent some small time looking around. Some Trippers came up from the south, and the men took care of them handily enough, but while they were finished them off, another, much larger group came from the north. The men fought, but they were overwhelmed by the odds. The last man to go down was Lieutenant Campbell. He emptied his gun into several Trippers who just took the rounds and kept coming. He went down with Three Trippers beating him to death, while a fourth tore open his guts.

"Christ Almighty. Thank God we put those walls up," Vega said, mostly to himself. He patted the tech on the shoulder. "Thanks for this...show."

Vega addressed the room. "Get the low fliers back; they're useless. Send up one of the bigger ones. I need a wider area searched."

"What are we looking for, sir?" one of the men asked.

"Start with that area, then circle out," Vega said. "Look for anyone not a Tripper. Don't bother with communities, just look for travelers. Let me know when you find one."

Captain Vega went back to his office. He pulled out a handful of letters and spent an hour addressing the families of the men he had sent over the wall. When that finished, he went over the files of the men he had left, and selected three of them. They weren't the best, but they were soldiers. And this time, he had an edge. He knew what the Trippers would do, and he also knew that bullets to the chest were useless. He wouldn't make the same mistake Campbell did.

For all his years of staring at the wall and hating what was on the other side of it, Captain Vega was doing something he never thought possible. He was going over the wall.

CHAPTER 45

"We're going to die."

"Probably."

"This is my fault, isn't it?"

"Yep."

"That's not nice."

"Nope."

"You can take them, can't you?"

"That's what I'm about to find out." I gave Kim a kiss on the top of her head and stepped out of my hiding spot. I was already drawing my bowstring back and getting a bead on the nearest Tripper I saw.

An hour ago, Kim and I had reached a small farm on the outside of a town. While I took care of the horses, Kim had decided to visit the town. She came back with a sack of supplies and a horde of Trippers on her trail. Kim and I took shelter in the stable while the Trippers wheezed and scrambled around outside. They didn't see us go into the stable, which was the only thing that saved us. What also saved us is we took shelter where all of our supplies and weapons were.

I fired my arrow and killed the Tripper, putting it into the back of his head. His companion, a small woman who was staring at a fencepost probably trying to figure out if she should hit it or not, went down on top of him with an arrow through her head. Those were the only ones in front of me, so my path was clear. I stepped forward, then turned around, searching for another target as I stepped carefully backwards. I didn't want to get too far, as it would be harder to hit targets that were too far away. If I could get them to march in a straight line that would help, but there was nothing here that would help me. In this part of the state, it was flatter than a tabletop.

I waited for a minute, but no Trippers came around. I waited a minute longer, and still no Trippers. I began to feel stupid standing in the snow with no one to kill.

I released the tension on my bow and picked up a stick next to my foot. I threw it up into the air and it came down hard on the roof of the stable. I had to laugh when I thought about what Kim's reaction to that might be.

I forgot about her reaction when a good-sized horde of Trippers came stumbling around the back of the stable, looking for whatever made the noise. They never figured out what the ruckus was, and I doubted they cared once they got a look at me.

I dropped two of them the second they came around into view, and another as he came around the other side. I kept doing this until there were about ten Trippers on the ground, and then I had to turn and run. They just started moving too many too fast in my direction. I pushed through the snow, looking to get to a little higher ground about fifty feet away.

Two Trippers, faster than the rest, started to outpace their peers. They came up behind me, somehow managing to stay in the path I had cleared. I pushed faster, and gave myself enough time to drop both of them. The rest used the time wisely, and I had them to worry about. I gained the hill and fired arrow after arrow. I hit most of them, missing a couple that stumbled at the right time or moved right before the arrow took them. Three of them reached the base of the hill when I ran out of arrows.

I held my bow out of the way with my left hand as I drew my gun with my right. The nearest Tripper, a huge man with dark red eyes, dropped as my first bullet took him in the face. The next Tripper, a teenager with a weird-looking haircut, died with another to his head. The last one fell and crawled up the hill, dying with an outstretched hand toward my boot.

I reloaded and went through the dead, collecting my arrows as I did. When I reached the back of the line, with the two I had originally killed, I found I had four more arrows than I started with. I guess Kim lent a hand after all.

I knocked on the door, waited a few seconds, then knocked again. I slowly opened the door, and put a hand out to the nose of Missy who was nervous about the sound of Trippers nearby. Judy was just looking at me with 'Where were you?' eyes, and Pumpkin couldn't care less.

Kim was holding my rifle, staring at the roof. She jumped when I touched her shoulder, and I had to be very fast to get the muzzle of my own gun out of my face.

"Josh! Jesus Christ on a stick! What the hell are you doing in there? There's a Tripper on the roof!" she whispered.

I don't know how I managed to keep a straight face, but I did. And the devil tempted me something fierce. I wanted so badly to play it out, but I likely might have gotten shot for my trouble. So I did the smart thing for a change and told Kim it was just a stick I had thrown onto the roof to make noise so the Trippers would come after me.

"Are you kidding? You scared the shit out of me! Don't ever do that again!" She swung her free hand at me and I stepped back. Judy stamped and blew behind me, and Kim knew better than to cause a bigger ruckus in a small area with three horses.

I apologized and spent the next fifteen minutes or so wiping off the arrows and putting them back in my quiver. I left the extra four out.

"Thanks for your help out there," I said.

Kim looked at me. "Those aren't mine."

CHAPTER 46

I sighed. "Nothing is ever easy." I picked up my rifle and went back outside, easing my way over to the side of the building. I used the sights of my rifle to scan the windows, and found the upstairs window was slightly open. I went back around to the other side of the stable and moved toward the front of the house. I kept all of the windows in sight, and I was ready to open fire if any of them twitched. None of them did, so I went up to the porch. I knocked on the door.

"Hello the house!" I said. Technically, I was in violation of convention by already being on the porch, but by being helped, the nuances were different.

No one answered. I waited for another five minutes, but no one showed up. I went back to the stable.

"We need to go. This is someone's place." I said.

"We just got here!" Kim said.

"And we just got refused entry," I said. "We need to go."

"Oh. They didn't even answer the door?"

"Nope."

"I'll saddle up the horses."

"I'll get the supplies and gear ready."

It was another convention of the times that if you were refused entry to the house or no one came to the door even when you knew they were home, you were to leave immediately. If you didn't leave, you were considered a threat and dealt with accordingly. I had figured the distance from the window to the Trippers was about seventy-five yards. They were all kill shots, and shooting from a high position wasn't easy. This was a place to leave alone.

We led the horses out and the sled worked as well as ever. I rode Missy over to the porch and dropped off the arrows. I didn't need them, and it was the best way to say we were sorry to have left a mess.

We headed back out onto the road and kept out heads pointed south. We'd find another place to stay. In the heart of Illinois, they were all over the place.

Harlem Avenue headed south and we stayed on it. It crossed I-57, but I wasn't interested in heading down that way again. It was too open, and not enough places to find supplies and shelter for ourselves and the horses. It was still winter, and I hadn't been planning on traveling until spring, but circumstances had forced my hand.

"Josh?"

Kim's voice broke me out of my revelations.

"What's up?" I figured she was interested in where we were going to spend the night.

"What will *I* do when we reach the southern community?" she asked.

That was a question I hadn't considered, but it was clear by Kim's tone that she had. I tried the old method of honesty. My dad always said that the truth was not always what people wanted to hear, but you could never be condemned for saying it.

"I don't know," I said. "I hadn't really thought about it that far ahead. I suppose you could take care of my horses for me."

I didn't have to look over to see Kim glaring at me. I could feel it. It was like a ray of sunlight that makes it through a cloudy day and warms your face. Only this warmth was followed by a small chill heading down my spine.

"Mr. Andrews. Please revise your statement." Kim's voice was about ten degrees colder than the air we were currently experiencing.

I laughed. "How about this one. If I am to be the sheriff of the southern communities, I will need a deputy to help me. You interested?" I said.

Kim's voice changed. "You mean it?" she said. "Really?"

"You're good with your bow; you'll need to find a gun and get good with it. Maybe a rifle would be easier to learn quickly. But you're smart, and you learn quickly," I said.

Kim smiled. "Why thank you, Josh. I was afraid you didn't notice."

"Except with baking. You seem to be going backwards in that area," I said.

I don't know how she did it, but suddenly a snowball hit me in the back of the neck. I didn't flinch as the snow went down the back of my neck. I refused to give her the satisfaction.

The sun set slowly, and we were in an area that was pure farm. Off in the distance, there was a line of trees covering the horizon. The fields were covered in tall grass, and there were a lot of trees making their way back. They weren't that tall, but then I knew exactly how old they were. They were born on the same day I was.

We moved along, and as we did, the sun went lower and lower. Out in the country, I wasn't as worried about Trippers, but they weren't the only predators. There were coyotes and wolves and who knew what else.

On the left side of the road, there was a large white building. It was next to a low ranch-style house. I turned Missy into the drive and dismounted. I held a hand up to Kim and moved toward the big white building. I walked around it, tapping on the sides and listening to see if there was a reply. When I heard none, I went over to the house and looked it over. There seemed to be no one inside, so I tapped on a few windows and didn't see anything come answering.

I went to the back door and tried to open it, but it was locked. The sliding glass door was open, however, and I went inside for a quick look.

The house was neat, but it was literally cleaned out. There was no furniture, no supplies, and no reason to think anyone had left this lace than for the simple reason that they were going somewhere else.

I went back outside to the long white building, and I forced a door open on the side. I didn't expect to see anything of use in here, but I needed to get the garage door open so we could set the horses up for the night. I was pleasantly surprised to find five stalls at the end of the garage, and even more surprised to find several large bags of feed. Our animals wouldn't know what hit their stomachs.

I went over to the animal entrance and opened the door, finding myself on the north side of the stable. I went towards the drive and stopped suddenly. A man was creeping along the side of the building like he didn't want to be heard. He was a large man, about my size, and he was holding a gun in his right hand as he crept forward. I drew my own gun and stepped behind him, keeping as silent as if I was stalking a deer.

Ahead of me, I could hear voices, and one of them was Kim arguing with a voice that didn't like what it was being told.

"You ain't got no call to throw down on us like that, Missy! No call at all! We was just coming by to see if we could spend the night in this big barn, and here you are telling us we can't. Why you need that big ol' gun, anyway? We can all be friends, why not? Don't even need to spend the night in the same part of the house. What you say?"

"I said, back off!" Kim shouted. "You make another move and I'll shoot!"

CHAPTER 47

"Why that ain't friendly at all, missy. Not at all. I was hoping you'd see things my way, and want to stay with us, for safety and all, but you pointing that rifle at me sure got me thinking we need to part ways."

The man in front of me reached the edge of the building, and he flattened himself even further. His right arm rounded the corner, and when he raised the gun towards Kim, I shot him in the butt.

The big slug slammed the man's pelvis into the building, and he shrieked like I had set him on fire. The gun flew from his hand, back towards me, and I picked it up and put it in my pocket. The man fell to the ground, clutching his wounded ass and his crushed nuts. I wasn't sure which of the wounds might hurt him worse.

I stepped around the man and into the general view of everyone on the west side of the garage. My gun was still in my hand, and I raised my other hand to calm down Missy, who was tossing her head and showing me the whites around her eyes.

"Easy, girl. It's just me. No need to worry." I spoke to the horse although I think I saw Kim calm down as well. I fixed my eye on the man who was speaking to Kim. He was a skinny man, although he was wearing enough clothing to make himself look bulky. I counted three shirts at least, a couple of jackets, and I could probably win a bet on whether or not he was wearing two pairs of jeans. He had dark hair tucked behind his ears and held in place with a baseball cap. His belt had a knife on the left side and a holstered gun on the right. There was a kind of pouch belted on there, too, but its purpose I could not discern.

Behind me, the man on the ground yelled and carried on something fierce, but no one moved. I suppose that had something to do with the fact that I was pointing my Colt at the skinny man's head. He had a second man behind him, and that person was doing his dead level best to keep his hands exactly at the same level as his ears. I think I saw him move his butt out of my line of fire, but I couldn't be sure.

"You okay?" I asked Kim, not taking my eyes off the leader.

"I'm fine. These assholes showed up out of nowhere and wanted our stuff. Then they wanted me!" Kim was showing her anger in her voice, and that was not doing well with our horses.

"Take the horses and the wagon around to the side. There's an animal entrance there I left open. There's a stall for each horse, and there's feed as well," I said. I wanted Kim to be doing something and calming herself down.

When she left, I faced the two men alone. I watched their eyes as Kim went past, and I could see the hunger in them for our supplies, our weapons, and our horses. I holstered my gun, a move that was not lost on Skinny. I kept my eye on him, figuring him to try some sort of move. He didn't, but that didn't endear him to me any.

"Time for you move on. Find another place to spend the night," I said.

Skinny looked at me and then at my holstered gun.

"Figured you to be a man to shoot first and ask questions later," he said. He looked at his companion on the ground, who had finally quieted down.

"I'm mostly a peaceful person," I said.

"Couldn't tell," Skinny said, looking over at his wounded man.

"Oh, don't get me wrong," I said with a small smile. "I prefer to go about my business peacefully, but that doesn't mean I don't remember how to be violent."

Skinny thought about that one. Whatever conclusion he reached didn't make him any happier. He motioned for the man behind him to help him, and the two of them went over to help their fallen man. They got him on a plank of wood from an old burn pile and carried him off, one end of the board sliding along the ground. He whimpered every time it hit a bump, but I wasn't sympathetic at all. He would have either shot or disarmed Kim had she been alone, and that would have been the better of the outcomes.

After they had gone, I went back to the stable. I told Kim we'd be staying in the garage tonight, as the two of them would probably try and pay us a visit tonight. They wouldn't shoot near the horses, so it was safer than being separated from the animals.

Kim was slightly shaken up, but she was better after feeding and watering the horses. We made a quick meal and found a place to sleep. I was actually tired from riding all day and I'm sure the horses were tired, too. Kim was asleep almost as soon as she lay down, likely coming down from the adrenaline rush she had when confronted by those men.

CHAPTER 48

It was very early in the morning when I woke. Kim was still sleeping, and it was really dark outside. I looked over at Judy and she was standing very still, with her ears pointed towards the house. I knew the men I had scared off would come back, I just wasn't sure when. And I figured they would assume we would be staying in the house. That was one of the reasons I decided to stay out here. Plus, Judy was the best alarm system when it came to strangers.

I slipped out of the stable and into the night. The moon was what my dad called a 'rustler's moon.' It was light enough to see by, but not light enough to get a good bead on someone trying to steal your cattle. I could see clearly enough, and I only needed to be able to hit a man-sized target. Even Kim could do that in this light.

I took my bow with me, and waited outside. I could see the front door, but they wouldn't see me until they stepped outside. The back door was around the corner, but anyone coming that way would be a target as well. The moonlight bathed the landscape in a bluish light, highlighting the snow and the tracks that led from the road to the house.

The tracks told me there were only two of them in there, so they must have either left their wounded somewhere or finished him off. I could see them doing either.

The front door opened and Skinny stepped outside. He had a gun in his hand and there was no mistaking what he planned to do with it. He held the door for his partner and closed it carefully, not wanting to make any noise. His partner moved toward the stable with his gun out and I put an arrow in his throat. He went down choking and kicking and Skinny had no idea what had happened. He raised his gun, looking for a target but my arrows were coming out of the darkness and he never saw it coming. It took him in the eye and he went down as well.

I suppose I might have felt bad about killing those two men, but no one could convince me that they had good intentions. I took my arrows out of their bodies and dragged their corpses over to the ditch. They died as they lived. Hard men in hard times. I wondered sometimes if I would meet an end similar to this one. I never thought about getting old. Maybe that was for the people on the other side of the wall.

I went back to the stable and made sure everyone was okay before I went back to bed. I watched Judy for a while, and when she relaxed, I knew I could go to sleep. If there was a third man out there, he'd likely see the bodies in the ditch and decide it wasn't worth his effort.

Morning came as a hard shaft of sunlight through a small eastern window. I was rolled up in my blankets and Kim was pressed up against my back. I could feel her breathing on the base of my neck and it was a nice feeling. Her arm was wrapped around my chest, holding me to her body. I must have been very asleep not to have felt her move in like that.

I pulled her arm off and she snuggled in tighter.

"Where are you going?" Kim asked sleepily.

"Need to look around," I said. "It's morning."

"Stay here. I'm cold."

"You can have my blanket."

"Okay." The arm disappeared under several blankets and joined a lump on the floor.

I chuckled as I got up. I guess my company wasn't really required after all. I fed the horses, and they were happy to get the change in diet. I checked the sleds and then pumped up some water for the horses and myself. This stable was very self-sufficient. The water pump had a hose attachment that moved water to the troughs in front of the stalls. That was a pretty neat trick. I filled a small bowl with water and splashed myself fully awake. The water wasn't frozen, but it was very close.

Outside, I saw that there had been some snow overnight. The tracks and blood that were there yesterday were covered in a thin layer of ice and snow. If I looked carefully, I could see the marks where the two men had fallen, and the drag lines I had made when I moved the bodies.

I walked toward the street, just looking around at the landscape. There were trees in the distance, and to the north, I could see the road as it moved up a hill. There was a strange lump in the road, and I walked carefully up to it.

As I got closer, I could see that it was not a strange lump; it was the outline of a man covered in snow. There were two dark areas of snow on the man. One near his rear, and other was near his head. I guess I knew what Skinny was going to do with his wounded comrade. I felt a lot less bad this morning about killing that one than I did last night, that's for sure.

The sky was a light grey in color, promising a gloomy day but not much else. The western sky was the same color, so today was going to be a good traveling day. I knew better than to try and announce my plans, because Dad always said that was a good way to hear God laugh.

When I got back to the stable, Kim was still sleeping, so I used the spare time I had to go through the house one more time. My dad always said that sometimes the obvious wasn't, and the hidden could be found if you looked for things that weren't where they were supposed to be. I had found more than one good stash of supplies when I went through some houses as a kid.

The house was still empty, but as I went through the rooms, something was bothering me. It was as if the house was too empty. I had read about people buying new homes and then selling their old ones, moving all of their things to another house. Maybe that's what happened here. I thought about it and decided that there was something else wrong here.

I went outside and circled the house, but nothing really stood out as being wrong. The backyard had a nice gazebo, and the rear of the house had a large porch that would be covered with the shade of a big oak tree that grew near the north side. On the south side, the window wells were mostly filled with snow from several snowfalls, and on the west side, the front of the house would get a nice sunset every evening.

I went back inside and looked around again. Then it hit me like a brick. Window wells meant a basement. I hadn't been down there. I went through the house but couldn't find a basement door. That was weird. I went outside and looked for an entrance, but there was none. I could see into the basement, and it looked like there might be something down there, but I couldn't tell for sure.

CHAPTER 49

Back inside, I looked more carefully, and in the kitchen, I found a drag mark on the tile that led to a wall. I pulled on a corner and stepped back as the wall swung away. It had been cleverly concealed right in plain sight. The edges of the wall had been hidden behind wood trim that covered the corners and crown molding hid the break in the ceiling. Behind the wall was the basement door.

I reached for the door handle, and as I turned it, I remembered to pull my gun. The stairs were covered in carpet, and I could see light coming in from the windows. I eased my way down, and when I reached the bottom, I just stood there. I couldn't believe what I was seeing.

The basement covered the full length of the house, and the people who lived here duplicated their home exactly. The living room, kitchen, bedrooms, everything was exactly the way it was upstairs, except for a small detail. This basement was full of everything that was supposed to be upstairs. Furniture, appliances, pictures, everything. They literally moved all of their belongings into a duplicate house.

In the bedroom, I found the occupants of the house. They were lying on the bed, holding hands. Their bodies were mummified, and on the dresser, there was a picture of an older man and woman holding hands. In the picture, they looked to be about seventy years old, and it was not hard to imagine the struggle they had in trying to survive the end of the world. I had to admire their ingenuity. They had nothing to build a wall with, so they retreated into a hole. Anyone coming into the house would see an empty place and figure the occupants long gone. I wondered how many times they had to listen to people like me or Skinny come into their house and stomp around like we owned it.

There was a plant by the window that looked like it had been there for just a little while. I looked it over, and after a minute of inspection, I knew what it was. My dad had shown it to me once when we were in the woods and his lesson stuck with me. The dried flowers and berries were a big clue, being dark purple in color, with large triangular leaves. It was Atropa belladonna, or more commonly known as deadly nightshade. Everything about the plant was deadly. Four berries could kill a child and ten could kill an adult. Eating a single leaf could kill an adult. Looking at the two on the bed, it seemed like they decided to head to the afterlife together before they got too old and frail to live in this world.

I left everything as I found it and went back upstairs. I closed the door and the wall, and left the house. It was one of the more strange things I had seen in a while.

I went back to the stable and found Kim had finally gotten up. I told her about the men I had killed and the house in the basement. She nodded at the first part and looked incredulous at the second.

"Seriously? The entire house in the basement?" Kim asked.

"Exactly the same," I said. "It must have taken them a while to build it and furnish it, but yeah, it was the same."

"And they were down there?" Kim said.

"Lying on the bed together. Looks like they poisoned themselves," I said.

"Wow. I want to go see, but I don't. Does that make sense?" Kim asked.

"It actually does. After I saw it, I kind of wished I hadn't. Made me kind of sad. They had nowhere to go and no way to defend themselves out here so they hid away. And when they realized that the world wasn't going to get better, they just decided to leave it," I said. "On the other side of it, I have to admit it was the most clever thing I have seen so far."

I finished my morning meal and packed up my bag. The horses seemed ready to move after a good night's rest, and I was grateful to move as well. This place had seen a lot of death. I had a hand in that death, truth be told, but it was there nonetheless.

I pushed the wagon out into the driveway and it slid a lot better over the snow than the floor of the stable. We walked the horses out, and this time, I hooked Missy up to the wagon. She needed to learn a new skill, too. Pumpkin resumed her place at the rear of the wagon, that skill was easy to learn.

CHAPTER 50

We headed south, staying on the road until we reached a small town. The road we were on ran along the outside of the town, where it met with another road heading south. We took the south road and stayed on it, quickly getting back to farm roads. I was trying to stay off the larger beaten paths just in case we were still being followed.

The roads we took were the roads that went around the farms in the area. I remembered seeing the same thing across the middle of the state. The roads covered a square mile of farmland. We saw a lot of empty fields, a lot of empty farmhouses, and a lot of empty barns.

Missy wasn't as agreeable to the wagon as Judy had been. She tended to wander all over the road, making the wagon slide back and forth. At one point, it almost fell off the road into the ditch.

As we moved south, the number of occupied areas increased. We passed several farms and homes that had survived the Trippers, and we traded for supplies at several of them. I traded off the guns I took from the three men I had killed, getting some dry goods for the road. One farmer had some jerked beef that he traded, and I thought it tasted better than venison, but Kim didn't like it. More for me, I guess.

We kept traveling south, deeper and deeper into farm country. None of the farms were worked as actual farms, but they did what they could with the equipment they had. Most of them had an acre or so of land they used as a garden, and they let the rest go to attract animals and birds. One man we met gave us some pheasant meat. For some reason, he had a lot of the birds and hunted them often. I hunted pheasant with my bow and stunned myself stupid when I actually hit one.

We stayed in homes that were abandoned, and it was good to see in this area that there were a lot more occupied homes than not. I had a fear that the men after me might try and kill the ones I met, but the people here were very self-sufficient, and wouldn't take that kind of thing lightly. I told each one that there might be some men following me, and to keep clear of them. It was the best I could do to try and keep them safer. I didn't tell them about the other side of the wall, and Kim asked me about it one day as we traveled.

"Don't you think they should know?" Kim asked.

"Sometimes I do, but then if I did, I would be condemning them to an early death," I said. "Let me ask you this. What if we told everyone we could find? They'd jump the wall and be killed piecemeal. If they did manage to get over in a group, they'd be hunted like I was. I got very lucky, but likely only because I was a single person. They set themselves up to keep mass migrations out."

"Still feels wrong not telling them," Kim said.

"Tell you what. The next people we meet, we'll ask them, and see what they say. If they seem likely to try it, let them go," I said.

Kim thought a minute. "Maybe we should be giving them the choice."

I shrugged. "Maybe. But let me ask you this. If I hadn't gone out and found a place to live, a safer place, would you have wanted to leave the life you built for yourself? We'd be asking people to leave their homes, only take what they can carry, and go try and make a life in a place eminently hostile to them. At least with the Trippers, we know what we're getting."

"You're right. We should have stayed where we were. It wasn't great, but we were doing pretty well," Kim said. She shivered in her coat. "I blame you for this."

I leaned over and pulled her close for a long kiss. "I'm glad you're here," I said, releasing her and letting her get her balance back. Pumpkin grunted at the weight shift.

Kim smiled. "I'm glad, too. I was just teasing."

We rode further, and as we did, I saw more and more signs that there had been a lot of Tripper activity in this area. I remembered coming up this way before, and that enormous Tripper horde that had kept me in a church for a while. I wondered where they were right now, and I hoped that I wasn't right in the middle of their territory. I thought I was too far north for them, but there was nothing that said they had to stay where they were.

CHAPTER 51

We spent the night in a house that was by a river, and by my reckoning, it was the Kankakee River. That meant the city of Kankakee was directly to our southwest. We were going to have to be careful in getting past that town. There was sure to be some Tripper activity there. We were far enough out that there shouldn't be a problem, but then you never knew.

Kim and I put the horses up in the large garage across the way from the house. Because there were Trippers nearby, I brought in with me my rifle, my Colt, and my bow. Kim had her gun and her bow, and we set up like we were in hostile territory. The front windows were covered with blankets from the bedroom, and the door was reinforced with a dresser. I scouted the back of the house and found that there was a path that led down towards the river, and this particular homeowner had a small pier that led a little into the river, and sitting on the pier was a small aluminum boat. It reminded me of the boat Trey and I used when we got very lost. I thought about that and it seemed so long ago.

The sun was not yet down, but we decided to go to bed early. I was tired from traveling, and I know Kim was. The horses were secure, and happy with their feed and river water.

We spread our blankets over a big bed in one of the bedrooms and climbed into bed together. We had slept close for enough weeks that it didn't even feel strange. Kim put her head on my shoulder and slept on her side while I wrapped her in my arm and slept on my back. Sometimes, she would put her leg over mine, but most of the time, she was asleep when she did that.

Tonight, she kept moving her arm, and when I looked down at her, she looked back. We stared for a long while, then she surprised me.

"I love you, Josh," Kim said.

I was floored. I had never imagined Kim thought about me that way at all, despite our hugs and kisses. I had a single response that had been in my head for a couple of years.

"It's about time. I love you, too," I said with a big smile. I hugged her close, and her hand kept moving around.

Kim looked at me seriously. "I think it's time we did something about it," she said.

I knew what she was talking about; I hadn't read only westerns in my time. I did read a couple of my mother's romance novels.

I knew this wasn't a time to be cavalier. I settled on honesty.

"I really have no idea what to do," I admitted.

Kim grinned. "You lay there; I'll take care of the rest."

And she did.

CHAPTER 52

I woke in the dead of night to a banging sound. I listened for a minute and realized it was coming from outside. It almost sounded like someone was screaming as well. I looked down and saw Kim was still sleeping, so she wasn't the problem. I slipped out of the bed and put my clothes on. It took a minute to find them since Kim took great delight in taking them off me and throwing them around the room. That was almost as much fun as watching her take her own clothes off. The memories of our lovemaking made it a little difficult to put my pants on; I had to concentrate on the noise outside.

Getting my rifle, I went into the front room and cautiously approached the front window. I hugged the wall and slowly opened the blanket, keeping my head back. I didn't see anything, then a Tripper came out of the darkness and walked past the window.

I ducked back, thankful the Tripper was walking away from me. I heard the banging again, and I realized that Missy must have smelled a Tripper or saw one walk by the window and was frustrated that she couldn't go out there and kill it. Missy never got over her need to kill the Trippers. She must have been hurt by one when she was younger. I wasn't worried about the other horses; there was enough space for them to stay out of the way, but her banging around would keep attracting Trippers. The big question I had was what was I going to do about it?

I went back to the bedroom and saw Kim was still sleeping. I didn't what was going to happen, so I decided to wake her up.

"Kim, there's Trippers outside," I said quietly in her ear.

Kim popped up from the bed, and I had a teasing glimpse of her naked form before she put her clothes on faster than I could draw my Colt.

"Trippers? Where? Are the horses okay?" Kim asked, belting on her gun.

"They're fine, but Missy is causing a ruckus and I don't know how to quiet her down. I can't go out there, and I sure don't want her attracting more," I said, getting my bow and quiver. Kim grabbed hers.

We went up to the front of the house and we could hear Missy making noise. I didn't know how many Trippers were out there now, so I decided to take a peek. I pulled aside the blanket and stared right into the face of a Tripper.

He saw me the same time I saw him, and he opened his mouth and let out a horrible wheeze I could hear through the glass. The next thing that came through the window was the Tripper's hands as he smashed it.

I jumped back as glass came flying, and Kim screamed. That scream was a clarion call to the Trippers, and suddenly there was wheezing all over the place. Where one Tripper was trying to get in the window, scrambling and clawing, suddenly there were ten, and more coming behind them.

"Go, go, go!" I said, pushing Kim ahead of me.

"Where I am going?" Kim yelled, heading towards the kitchen.

"Out the back!" I said.

"What if there's Trippers?" Kim asked.

"Then we kill them, but we can't stay here!" I said. I reached the back door first as the sound of Trippers moving through the house followed us. I went through the door and barreled into a small Tripper.

I managed to keep my feet, but the Tripper went sprawling in the snow. She got up soon enough and came at me, raging and grasping. I stepped to the side and pushed her past me, tossing her into the house. Kim closed the door, and we left the Trippers where they were.

Our respite was short lived as the back door exploded outward with the pressure of dozens of Trippers.

"Run!" I said, drawing an arrow and killing the nearest Tripper. As it was only ten feet from me, it wasn't a difficult shot.

"Where?" Kim asked, turning away.

I had an idea. "The pier! Go there!" I said, pushing Kim along.

"I don't know where it is!"

I forgot that part. "Come on!" I said. I grabbed her hand and pulled her along. We ran toward the water and then along its edge. More Trippers were coming around the side of the house and several were still coming through the back door.

Kim and I hit the pier at a dead run and we reached the boat. I flipped it over and told Kim to get in. Trippers reached the pier in a pile of teeth, fists, and rage. I shoved the boat across the snow and jumped in as we landed in the water. Kim yelled as the boat dipped very low in the river, but it righted itself and we moved across the hundred feet of water until we landed on the other side. Kim grabbed some tree branches over the water to pull us in, and I shoved us forward until we were able to get out without getting wet.

I pulled the boat up and Kim and I scouted the area. It turned out we hadn't really crossed the river at all, we just happened to be on a small island in the river. On the other side, Trippers were falling into the water and were sinking out of sight. Several were standing on the edge of the water, looking over like they wanted to take a swim. Thanks to the trees, Kim and I were largely invisible.

"Well, we may lose some arrows, but I think a bit of target practice is in order," I said.

Kim laughed. "You sure know how to show a girl a good time."

"I thought I did that earlier," I said.

"Oh, God," Kim said.

We shot the small horde of Trippers that were standing on the pier and on the lawn. I shot ten of them, and Kim shot eleven. We waited in the cold for about fifteen minutes, and when the Trippers didn't show up, we figured the coast was at least much clearer than it was.

"How are we going to get across?" Kim asked.

"Well, wait here," I said. I took the boat and did pretty much the same thing I did before, only this time Kim wasn't with me.

I made it to the other side, pulling myself across the last few feet by grabbing the leg of a dead Tripper that was half in the water. I circled the house and went through it, finding only one Tripper that I killed easily. He was stuck in the window and not going anywhere.

Missy had calmed down when the Trippers went away, and the other horses looked at me like I was crazy. I took an extension cord off the wall and went back to the pier.

I tied the extension cord to my arrow and shot it over to Kim. After that, it was easy to send the boat over and pull her back.

We took our stuff out of the house and went over to the garage with the horses. There was a small office space in there and there was room enough to sleep. I was suddenly so tired I couldn't even stand up. As soon as the blankets were on the ground, I fell down and just closed my eyes. Kim joined me and I think I was asleep before she was.

Missy was quiet, so the Trippers were gone, at least for now.

CHAPTER 53

After a lot of deliberation, we figured it may be safe by now to hit the highway. I had two reasons for this: one the highway was safer to travel than the back roads, being fenced-in on two sides, and two, I wasn't exactly sure where the massive horde might be and I didn't want to find myself in the middle of it with no place to go.

We followed the road towards Kankakee, and I rode with my rifle across my lap. I wasn't taking any chances as we got closer and closer to what once was civilization. Kankakee was a big place, and the likelihood of Trippers hanging out was pretty high.

The road took us past a tall building that had a lot of windows. It looked like an office building, but not exactly the same. I asked Kim about it.

"That's a condo building. There's lots of them up north," she said.

"What's a condo building?"

"That's where there's a bunch of little homes all stacked on top of each other. One and two bedrooms, usually with a living room and a kitchen," Kim said.

I looked at the building and just shook my head. I couldn't imagine for the life of me living in a place where I couldn't step out my back door and see my own land. That was just how I was. That stacked up living was just nuts. I said so to Kim.

She laughed at me. "You'd hate the city, then."

No need to tell me, I was already there. I had no desire whatsoever to see a major city. I was curious, though. If I could see Chicago from a safe distance, I'd take a peek.

We took an on-ramp carefully to the highway, working our way around a few wrecked and rusting cars. There were more on the highway, which told me Kankakee wasn't the best place to try and find a place for two refugees and three horses with a wagon.

The sun arced across the sky and we kept moving south. I made Missy pull the wagon again because she was naughty last night. Judy was more attuned to the environment. I tried getting Pumpkin more alert, but I think she was a lot older than we thought she was. Nothing seemed to phase her; she just took it as it came.

We got off the road at the exit of Ashkum, and went west on County Road 2. There was a farmhouse just down the road, and we opted to stop there. There was a nice barn behind the house, a big, old-fashioned one. I hailed the house, and Kim waited with the horses while I did my usual checking. Everything seemed okay, so we put the horses in their own stalls, fed them with the feed we still had and some hay that was up in the loft. Water was a little trickier, but we managed to pull up some from a well that had been covered over with a wood plank.

The farmhouse was a two-story affair that had seen some better days, but it was tight and it was dry. Inside there was every bit of evidence that the people who lived here still did. There was food in the pantry, clothes in the bedrooms, and I found a shotgun in a small niche by the door. Down in the basement was a collection of bows and targets. I looked them over but none was as good as the one I already had. I took the arrows, though, since you could never have enough of them. The guy who lived here was a big fan of broadhead arrowheads. I found boxes of them, and I brought a couple upstairs. They would be good if we got a shot at a deer.

Kim raided the food, and managed to put together a decent meal. As we ate, we talked about the farmhouse.

"Where do you think the owners are?" Kim asked.

"No idea," I said. I was planning on leaving them a couple of silver coins for the food and lodging.

"Think they will be back before dark?"

"No idea. This doesn't look like a very secure place. They must have either a hiding place or they just run when the Trippers come," I said.

We went upstairs and got ready for bed. I looked out the window and something in the yard didn't look right. I looked again and called Kim over.

"I think I found our hosts," I said.

"Oh, dear," Kim said.

Out in the yard, there were two human-shaped lumps in the snow. One was out by a building and the other was closer to the house. They were facing each other, and it wasn't hard to figure out that one had been attacked and the other had tried to help. Bad luck. Chances were it had happened recently.

"Well, we can try and bury them tomorrow. Least we could do for their post-mortem hospitality," I said.

"Ugh. You can do that. I hate moving bodies," Kim said.

"Okay, but you have to take care of the horses," I said.

"That's not fair. Judy doesn't like me," Kim complained.

"Grab some corpse then," I said.

"Arrgh!" Kim tackled me onto the bed. I wasn't sure if she was taking my suggestion literally and was going to kill me or she was mad about my making her work tomorrow. Either way, we got into bed, which helped, since I was actually very tired.

CHAPTER 54

I found a pick and a shovel in the work shed, and went to work in the early morning. I had gotten out of bed before Kim awakened, and I spent some time with the horses. Judy was glad to see me, and Missy was too. I fed them, gave each a good combing, and let them out into the small pasture behind the barn. It was fenced-in, so I wasn't worried about them wandering.

I dug a single grave for the both of them, and took blankets out of a closet to cover them in. I placed them side-by-side and filled the grave. I did not look at either one of them, as I had seen Tripper work before.

As I buried them, and finished covering the grave, I had to wonder how they got caught outside the way they did. The house was very sturdy; in the light of day, I could see that it was more of a fortress than a house. The door was solid, and there were shutters that actually closed up the windows. They were solid as well. I saw that when the shutters were closed, there were no edges for Trippers to grasp; it was a smooth wall. I had to admire the ingenuity of the solution. They didn't need more walls; they just made the ones on their house impregnable. The only flaw in the plan was you had to be inside the walls to be safe.

Kim and I had breakfast, and I spread the map of Illinois I had out on the table.

"Here we are," I said, finding Ashkum. I drew a line all the way down to Marion. "And here is where we want to go."

Kim looked at the distance. "Good heavens, that'll take a month."

"About that much, maybe more," I said. "On the plus side, it'll be warmer every day we get closer to spring."

"Bonuses all around," Kim said. "How was the burying?"

I caught the change in subject and played along with it. "They didn't object," I said. I looked Kim straight in the eyes. "Something on your mind?"

Kim looked out the window and then down at the map. She traced a finger down the border between Illinois and Indiana. "I don't know. Maybe I wonder if we should try our luck on the other side. With your skills and my memories, we could get out of here, make a life." Kim looked at me.

I shook my head. "For how long? At some point, we would make a mistake. Then it would be all over. The people over there don't want us. They walled us in and let us die. They didn't care. I've seen them kill."

Kim sighed. "I know. But I wonder sometimes."

"Tell you what. Once we're settled in down south, there's nothing saying that we can't find a safe way over and visit from time to time when we want to," I compromised.

Kim brightened immediately. "Really?"

"It would take some doing, but I think it could be done," I said. "Might even be fun to play both sides."

Kim hugged me and we set about preparing for our next step in our journey. We decided to spend a couple of days here, and give the horses a good rest. I took my bow and went into the woods across the street, and had good luck getting two rabbits.

Kim practiced with her bow, shooting from longer distances. I showed her how to use the Winchester, and she thought she might want a rifle of her own. I told her she could have the shotgun, it wasn't being claimed by anyone. She liked that idea until she shot it; even I didn't like the kick on that mule. We left that one where it was.

CHAPTER 55

On the second day, we decided to get moving. The day was very bright and I could tell the horses were starting to itch for the trail. Judy was a horse born for the explorer, and I wasn't cruel enough to keep her penned up. Missy did whatever Judy did, only with a healthy dose of cussedness. That was a word I found in my westerns and it fit her to a T.

I-57 was a long, lonely stretch of road, and I found it hard to imagine that people used to drive all over the country on roads like this. I'd have been bored out of my mind, constantly wondering when I would arrive at my destination. At least on horseback you had the advantage of moving slowly, taking in the scenery. Of course, in the middle of Illinois, there wasn't much to the scenery, but here we were.

Towards the end of the day, we decided to get off the road and make a camp for the night. We got off the highway at some county road that didn't even have a name. There was a house to the east and we started for it. In the distance, there was a large farm operation, which would be our second choice if the house didn't pan out.

I had my eye on the house when Kim turned and looked at out back trail. She did that a lot, probably from her days of running from the Trippers all the time.

"What's that?" she asked.

I looked back, shading my eyes from the setting sun. It looked like two large boxes were sitting on the road behind us, about five hundred yards back.

"Not sure," I said. I hadn't remembered seeing those boxes when we got off the road, but then I was concentrating on getting Pumpkin up a steep hill while pulling a sled.

"It's weird they would be in the road like that," Kim said. "Should we go see?"

"We can check it out in the morning," I said, leading the horses into the driveway of the house.

I got off Missy and led her and Pumpkin over to the large barn near the house. The house was old, with a large tree in the front yard. There was a wind break that had to be a hundred years old, and the outbuildings looked like their best days were long behind them. The barn looked much newer, and it took a moment to check it out and get the two horses put away and the wagon as well.

I went back outside and Kim was still sitting on Judy. Her head was down on her chest, like she had fallen asleep. I went over to her and put a hand on her leg.

"Hey, sleepy, you can do that inside," I said, jokingly.

Kim said nothing; she just slumped over and fell off Judy into my arms.

"Whoa!" I said, catching her. I put her on the ground and then I noticed her chest was covered in blood.

"Kim? Kim? *KIM!*" I yelled, shaking her and checking her for life. I found no pulse at her throat or her wrist.

"No, No, *NOOO!*" I raged, not knowing what to do. I pulled my gun and looked around. I didn't see anyone anywhere. I hadn't heard any shot, either. Judy stamped her feet, and then there was a sickening sound of metal striking flesh. Judy let out a deep groan, then slumped to her knees. She lay down slowly, putting her head out. I reached out a hand and Judy breathed her last onto my palm.

I roared in pain and anger, my heart torn at what had just happened. In the space of a few seconds, I lost the woman I loved, and the horse that had been my loyal companion for most of my life. I couldn't breathe, I couldn't see.

I carried Kim over to the house and laid her down gently. Her eyes were closed and she looked like she was sleeping, but I knew she would never wake up in this world again. I ran over to the barn and grabbed my heavy Savage rifle off the wagon. I already had my bow and Colt, but I needed to figure out what the hell had just happened and who was responsible.

My first thought was the two boxes we had seen on the road, and so I circled back around the house to try and get a look through the wind break. I had no idea where shots might come from, or if I would even hear them. I stayed low, easing through the grass like I was stalking someone.

Which, as I thought about it, I was. My face was impassive, but tears ran down my cheeks as I thought about Kim and Judy. I was sick at heart, but my pain was balanced by the nearly overwhelming desire to kill, to smash, to destroy. I wanted to cause pain, I wanted to hurt something, I wanted to hear someone beg for their life.

I wanted vengeance.

CHAPTER 56

I looked through the trees and down the road, and saw the boxes were moving closer. I could see now they weren't really boxes, but rather boxy trucks. They were well armored, and the armor extended nearly to the ground, causing them to look the way they did.

I took aim at the driver's window of the nearest one and fired, sending a bullet through the glass. The large vehicle swerved suddenly, running south off the road. The truck behind it stopped and two men got out, running to the side and taking cover behind it.

Four more men got out of the truck I had shot and joined the other men. I moved from my position to a new one, and glad I did. Three of the men began firing their weapons, neither of which made a sound louder than a handclap. It was no wonder I hadn't heard the shots that killed Kim and Judy.

They weren't the only ones who could shoot quietly. I pulled my bow and measured the range carefully. There was no wind, and I pulled the bow back. I had to relax and try again twice due to my hands shaking. I took a deep breath, steadied myself, and loosed the arrow. I backed away from the tree and moved again.

There was a scream and a man fell to the ground, an arrow sticking out of his face. He didn't move, and I knew I had killed him. I was using my compound bow, so the arrows were little more than black streaks through the air.

More bullets ripped the trees, and I had to take cover behind a larger one, but not before I shot another arrow, this time without aiming. I hit something metal, but no one else screamed. The bullets hit the house, and I hoped the horses were okay. Suddenly, the firing stopped, and I heard a voice calling out.

"Hey, Runner! You still alive?"

I didn't respond. I lay down on the ground and sent another arrow roughly in the same direction as the other one. It struck something metal and there was a healthy round of cursing.

"You're a dumb son of a bitch, you know that?" the voice called again. "I figured you'd have disappeared after you found the bodies of that couple at the farmhouse. But you buried them and walked right towards us."

I lay back and cursed myself for a damn fool. I never checked those bodies for any wounds. I just assumed they had been killed by Trippers. They had been tracking us the whole time. They just kept the spies out of sight.

The voice continued. "Just so you know, you bastard, you hauled me out of a very comfortable base on the other side of the wall and made me come to this shithole. You killed my men, shot down my drones, and probably infected people in the civilized world with who knows what. We had to test that whole high school for the Tripp virus, you asshole!"

While he was talking, I stood back up, and moved back towards the house. Once around back, I ran for the barn and grabbed my heavy rifle again. I went over to the trees and found an opening to see what they were doing.

"Just so you know who killed you and your woman, my name is Captain Vega, and I killed dozens of you seventeen years ago when the wall first went up. And by God, I will kill you."

There were three more of them; two were pointing rifles in my direction and the other was sitting in the truck. I lined a shot up and exhaled slowly, bringing the trigger back slowly. The rifle bucked, and there was suddenly only one man holding a rifle.

"You son of a bitch!" the man yelled and suddenly bullets ripped all around me. I dove for the ground and crawled back towards the house. I ran around to the other side and waited as I heard the truck's engine suddenly roar. I lay down to present a smaller target and the truck raced past the house. A man on the outside was firing towards the house and the other was driving. I shot at the man firing, and cursed when my gun went empty. I think I hit him, because he jerked suddenly and scrambled inside.

The truck rolled out of sight, and I could do nothing but watch it leave. I did get a good look at the driver, and I knew I would remember him.

When the adrenaline wore off, I went over to Kim and I just cried for a long time. I kept telling her I was so sorry for my mistake and for not protecting her. I took her inside and lay her on a bed. I covered her with a blanket and went out to the barn. I calmed the horses down, and took them out to let them walk a bit. They both went over to Judy and smelled her, nudging her a little bit. Judy was beyond responding, and eventually, the horses knew what I did and they walked away, saying their goodbyes. Missy reared and neighed, and Pumpkin just blew several times.

I knelt down by my old friend and put my hand on her neck. I couldn't do anything but shed fresh tears that splashed down on her hide. Judy had been with me for so long she was family. She was the last link I had to my home and now she was gone. And for what? I just didn't understand why.

I dug a grave for Kim and lay her in it, covering it with dirt and laying stones over the top. I put together a cross to mark her grave, knowing it wouldn't last long in the winters here, but maybe with luck, it might. I hung her bow on the cross; I figured she might need it in the afterlife if the Trippers had crossed over.

I used the other horses to drag Judy to the ditch, then I spent a day burying her as well. She deserved better than just to be left out to rot. I covered her in stones and lay a marker for her as well. She was my friend and savior more times than I could count, and I owed her a debt.

CHAPTER 57

I spent the next few days trying to figure out what I was going to do. I couldn't just let this go. My world had been destroyed, and someone had to answer for it. I looked to the east every morning and a growing hatred started in my heart. I wanted to hurt that world out there, I wanted to teach them a lesson they would never forget. I wanted to take their world away from them.

The truck had stayed where it was since I had shot the driver, and I had not bothered to bury the men I had killed. I couldn't care less what happened to them. I took their weapons and gear, and whatever I found useful, but they were worth less to me than the wood I burned for fuel.

One day, I went into the truck and found a load of supplies, food, and weapons. There was a lot of ammunition for the guns, and I felt like I had hit the motherload. I tried starting the truck, but it was dead. Apparently, the arrow I put into it had done something to the engine and killed it. That wasn't too much of a problem. I didn't know how to drive, anyway. There was one item that was interesting. It was a small box that had a small keypad on it like an old telephone. On the back was taped a handwritten note with some numbers and names on it. I wasn't sure what that meant but it seemed important so I held on to it.

I was reluctant to leave the house and barn, since it was where Judy and Kim were buried, but I knew I couldn't stay here forever. I had a plan, and it was going to take some work, but I really had nothing else to do, and no one to live for. Revenge was my family now.

I had one weapon to use against that world, and I planned on making it painful.

CHAPTER 58

After two weeks in the same place, it was time to get moving. The weather was starting to warm up and there was a feel of spring in the air. The Trippers were going to be more active and hungry as the weather got better, which suited me just fine.

I needed to move faster than I had in coming down here, so I decided to alter the wagon a bit. The sleds were in decent shape, but I wanted the horses to be able to move along further each day and still be able to move the next. To that end, I used some lumber I found in the barn and made a harness system where both horses could pull the wagon.

The day we pulled out, I said my goodbyes to Judy and Kim, and I made a promise to them both that their deaths would not be unavenged. I had it to do. I didn't just want revenge. I wanted a reckoning, as my western books called it.

The wagon worked pretty well, although it was a bit rough at first. Missy wanted to pull in another direction sometimes than Pumpkin did, but Pumpkin surprised me with how she kept Missy in line. It was almost as if she was stepping up into the role that had been vacated by Judy.

The horses trotted along, and we made at least twice the distance that we had made traveling before. We weren't going south, however; we were going north. What I needed wasn't where I was going; it was where I had been. All thoughts of Southern Illinois were gone from my head. I had a new plan, and the job and new life were going to have to wait.

I had a man to kill, and his name was Vega.

CHAPTER 59

It took us two weeks of hard travel, but we made it back to the homestead. Everything was exactly as it had been left, except there was a great big hole that Judy and Kim used to fill. The house felt empty, even though it was still filled with my things. I spent a lot of time just walking around the house, and walking around Kim's house. There was a slight smell of bread in the air at her house, and it caused more than one tear to escape my eyes.

I unpacked my weapons and the weapons of the men who came after me. I spent a week familiarizing myself with one of their rifles, firing it, and getting used to working it. It seemed flimsy compared to my other rifles. The stock was plastic, and the receiver felt like it was made out of a lighter metal than steel. But it shot well and held a lot of bullets that were accurate out to three hundred yards. The short scope on top of the rifle was useful, too. Against a horde of Trippers, I think I could hold my own as long as I had enough bullets. And thanks to the truck I cleared out, I had over three thousand rounds of ammunition, more than I have ever had for a gun.

I loaded ten of the thirty-round magazines and packed them into a backpack. The rifle had a sling that held the gun to my chest, so I was still able to carry my bow and my Colt was still stuck to my hip.

I spent several days making arrows, and these were special arrows. I used some of the gunpowder I had for reloading, and took some practice shooting the heavier arrows. I had a use for these, and I hoped that what I was going to do with them was going to be successful. I also made a quick run to the east, and that was a very enlightening experience.

The last thing I needed was a boat. Instead of randomly hunting for one like Trey and I had done, this time I knew where to go to get one. There was a campground not far from here and they had canoes. That would serve.

I took Missy out and we went south. About ten miles out, I came upon the campground. It was little more than a collection of small cabins around a lake that wasn't more than three acres. Kim told me once that the difference between a pond and a lake was depth. I argued that if I had a hole that was only three feet square but forty feet deep it would be a lake? Kim had said yes, and I thought she was crazy.

When I thought about her, my eyes turned south, and I hoped she forgave me for making the mistakes I did.

The big shed had the boats and I took one of the canoes off the rack. I remembered to grab a paddle and tossed it in the boat. I wrapped rope through one of the braces and tied the other to my saddle horn. Missy was not too thrilled about pulling the canoe, but she didn't fight me more than a little.

On our way back, we ran into a Tripper coming out of a barn, and Missy started for it. She jumped for it and I tried to rein her in, but she raced forward again. I yanked hard on the reins and Missy stopped short. The canoe swung around and hit the Tripper in the knees. The infected person tumbled down, smacking its head on the side of the road. It stayed down, and I walked Missy away from it. The blood coming out of the Tripper's head was dark red, and it wasn't going to get up from that.

Back home, I laid out all of my gear and made sure I had what was needed. I was going to be playing with fire, and I surely didn't want to get burned.

CHAPTER 60

The water looked really, really cold as I put the canoe in. I had brought it out toward Lemont as opposed to going north, since there was a lot of Tripper activity that way. I got chased back to my house and spent three days shooting arrows into Trippers. The bonfire from that group was a very large one. I left the horses behind, as I didn't want to get them into trouble, and I didn't plan on being gone longer than a day. I wasn't looking for a fight, just wanted to get things moving. I picked a day when the wind was blowing from the east; I needed that for this to work.

I got into the water and started paddling north. The hills of the river valley rose on either side of me as the silent barge loaders stood sentry to the river. The waterway split north and east, and I took the right fork. I had studied my maps and knew where this waterway was going to take me.

A length of barges waited on the shore, patiently in line for loads that will never come. The barges were the last thing I saw on the canal for a while, the edges of the water becoming completely lined with trees. It was actually kind of nice.

The miles flowed past, and the bridges became more frequent. I could see many houses and buildings, and I decided to make a start. I tied up the canoe at the edge of the river and carefully made my way inland. There was a huge subdivision south of me and I could already see Trippers wandering around. I took my bow and one of my special arrows out. I lit the long fuse and drawing the bow back I launched the arrow as far as I could. The fuse fizzed the whole way, and the arrow sailed out of sight.

The explosion was a hell of a lot louder than I expected, and every Tripper in sight started in that direction. They came out of the houses and they appeared from every direction. They all wandered toward the place where the explosion had come from.

All was well. I made my way back down the bank of the river to the canoe, and pushed off again. That noise had echoed down the canal, and I was sure it was starting some movement on the north side of the water as well.

At the next stop, I launched an explosive on the north side of the river and a flare on the south side. I alternated on both sides of the river, figuring if nothing else I was drawing them towards the water.

I paddled a little further than before, wanting to put some distance between the masses. I parked it near another bridge and made my way up the bank. There weren't any Trippers in sight, so I launched an arrow into the buildings to the south. The arrow sizzled out of sight and then nothing.

"Are you kidding me?" I said. I pulled out another arrow and put it to the bow. I lit it and aimed about where I had put the other one. I was just about to release when the first one when off. I stepped back, startled, and slipped a little down the bank. I launched the arrow straight up into the air.

"Oh, shit!" I said. I slid down the bank and pushed the canoe out into the river. I paddled under the bridge and stayed there, waiting for the arrow to fall. There was a huge explosion right above the bridge, rocking the water and causing my ears to ring.

The explosion was followed by a loud string of wheezing, and a Tripper falling into the water right in front of my canoe. The wake rocked the boat, and I waited a second before another one fell into the water.

"Not what I need right now, guys," I said, paddling over to the other side of the river. I dug in the water and pushed forward getting out from under the bridge. Another Tripper landed in the water behind me, causing the canoe to shoot forward a bit.

This wasn't as easy of a trip as I had hoped. I had been canoeing before, but it had been with my dad, and he basically controlled the boat while I was more of just a participant in the exercise. But the basics were pretty easy, and if you weren't an idiot, you could figure it out.

I paddled faster, and I could see the shoreline and bridge filing with Trippers. There were a lot of them, and I was hoping to get more. I had a bunch of bomb arrows and I planned on using them all. That is, if I didn't manage to kill myself first.

I kept moving and shooting, and I reached a point where I had to shoot from the canoe. The banks of the canal were too steep to climb out, and there wasn't any place I could tie the boat up to. But it was a good thing, as I moved deeper and deeper into the populated areas. The city was very close, and the canal widened considerably. The sun was up high, and the area was very clear. I sent one sailing into the streets, and I could hear the echo of the blast reverberating among the buildings. I listened for the telltale wheezing that told me the Trippers were on the move, and I went down to the next spot.

When I was down to my last four arrow bombs, I began to look for a place to park the canoe. The next part of the plan was a little more dicey. I paddled hard until I reached the spot where I-57 crossed the river. I jammed the canoe into the underbrush at the river's edge, grabbed my bag, and adjusted my quiver and guns. I had a feeling that the explosions were causing a few of those drones to come to the area, and I wanted to take a couple of those out as well. I carried one of the rifles I took off the men down south, and it had a decent scope on it.

I ran up the steep embankment, slipping and climbing in the dirty snow. My hands were cut and bruised, and I almost went sliding back down the way I had come, but at last, I pulled myself over the edge of the highway. To the north, I could see hundreds of figures milling about, and out over the expanse of homes, I could see hundreds more milling about. If I had to guess, I had put a few thousand in motion.

I moved fast, knowing I didn't have a lot of time. The air was full of wheezing, and I was sure a great number of Trippers from Chicago were on the move. Trippers were weird that way. They would stand around and stare at nothing, but if one of them had an interest in something, suddenly they all had an interest in it. It was almost as if they had a way of communicating with each other. Who knows; they were evolving and getting more dangerous. Maybe they could talk to each other. If so, then I was doing the right thing.

I moved with the rifle out, and a couple of times I had to shoot a Tripper that hadn't quite made it to where the noise had been coming from. If I had done the job right, I had agitated and put into motion Trippers from both sides of the river. The last thing I needed to do was draw them all south. I shot another arrow behind me and ran as it exploded. I wanted to be another half mile away before I sent my next one. I was getting to the really dangerous part, and it was going to be a big matter of timing.

CHAPTER 61

Five hours later, as the sun was setting, and after three explosions punctuated the evening festivities, the time saw me on Interstate 80 heading east. Behind me, coming from I-294, and from I-57, were literally tens of thousands of Trippers. Maybe a few hundred thousand. I didn't stop to count. But they filled the streets from one side to the other, and these were ten-lane highways. Their wheezing and growling was awful to hear, but I wasn't finished with them yet. That wheezing pulled in every Tripper from every subdivision we passed, calling them to us like a siren song of death and pain.

I walked and jogged to keep ahead of them, and I knew we had ten miles to go. The snow was helping me more than it was helping them. I was able to keep my footing better than the Trippers did, and when one went down, it always took out the next three behind it. But they always scrambled to their feet and kept moving, following the herd. I wondered as I walked if the ones in the middle had any idea what was going on, or if they just followed the crowd.

As I walked, I thought about Kim and Judy, and it helped with my resolve with what I was about to do. I needed the darkness, and the clouds were most obliging, darkening the sky after a brilliant sunset.

Ahead of me in the dark rose an even darker mass, and I ran further ahead to gain some distance. I pulled the final special arrow out of my pack. I had one shot at this and I couldn't miss. I could see the small grey box on the side of the wall, and I knew I was in the right place.

I stood back from the wall and shot my arrow over it. Attached to the arrow was a knotted rope, and the arrow had a small grappling hook tied to the end of it, instead of a field point. The arrow sailed over, and I carefully pulled it back. The hook caught and I was up and climbing in an instant. Behind me, the horde kept advancing, and in the darkness, I scurried over the wall.

I repositioned the grappling hook to the other side, and then climbed back down. I stayed in the darkness and moved carefully east. When I found my preparations, I checked to make sure they were still in place, and ready to go.

I had cut four full sections of fence away, and placed a line of gunpowder off into the distance toward the fence. When everything looked okay, I ran back to the wall. I climbed back up, and looked out over the other side. The road was filled with Trippers, and they were looking for what had brought them out here. Some of them started to wander away, so I shouted down at them to get their attention.

You would have thought I had just announced a free dinner. Hungry- and hate-filled eyes stared up at me, and I pulled the second to last trick out of my bag. It was the little controller with the strange numbers that I had pulled from the truck down south. I had been looking at a map of the state when I remembered the controller. The little piece of paper with names and codes seemed odd until I compared it to the map. The names and numbers were street names and county roads, and the codes were the ones to open the gate for that section of the wall.

I entered the code for I-80 and pressed the green button. There was a rumbling in the wall beneath me, and suddenly the Trippers were moving through the wall. I watched them go past, and on the other side, they began to spread out.

I pulled the last arrow out and struck it against the ground. The flare burned brightly and I shot it towards the gunpowder line. The gunpowder sparked like a beacon and flamed off into the distance, catching the sticks and twigs I had placed in the powder on fire. The line of flame went off into the distance and the Trippers followed it. They headed right for the opening in the fence.

It took the entire night for the massive horde to go through the gate. I just lay on the wall and took a nap, as I was pretty tired. When I woke, it was just starting to get grey in the eastern sky. There were still a few Trippers walking along the highway, and after another two hours, the last of them wandered through the gate. I hit the red button on the controller and felt the gate close

BORN IN THE APOCALYPSE 3

beneath me. I figured there were still several Trippers in the area, so I started walking south on top of the wall.

If I had to guess, there were probably half a million to over a million Trippers that went through that gate last night. The people who lived in the towns nearest the wall wouldn't have any idea what was coming. I felt a small pang of regret at what they were going to go through, but it was tempered by the knowledge that they left us to die, and would kill us if we tried to save ourselves by crossing the wall.

I kept walking, and in a little while, I started to hear the sounds of the drones. They were buzzing around soon enough and one came over to take a look at me. I waved and it hovered just out of pistol shot. I reached into my pack and pulled out a piece of paper. I had written on it with large black letters, and I held it up for a minute to give the drone a good chance to see what it said.

After that, I tossed the sign over the wall and pulled up my rifle. The drone sped up out of range and flew away. It was a good time for me to drop off the wall. I was nearing where I wanted to be, anyway.

I climbed down the wall and started walking back towards my house. The sun on my back felt great, and I kept a watchful eye out for any activity. I was back on the road I had once traveled with my father just five years ago, but it seemed like a lifetime.

I spent the remainder of the day walking back, and I didn't see a single Tripper. I knew there were more to the north, and I know I didn't get all of them to walk through the gate. But I had the controller, and there was one more horde I wanted to get out of the state.

CHAPTER 62

Four weeks later, I was standing on the wall at night again, this time much further south. I had packed up Pumpkin and Missy, and we had headed this way. I had stopped at the graves of Judy and Kim to pay my respects, and after that, we went hunting. The Trippers made it really easy, since they were near the wall anyway. I only needed to give them a small push in the right direction.

This time, the Trippers were through in only three hours, and I closed the gate after them. I watched them walk away into the darkness, chasing the flare I had sent through the gate again. That was my last flare, so it was the last time I was going to be sending Trippers out of the state. I knew there were more, but the codes on the controller only listed roads to the north. This was the last gate listed on the paper.

I walked along the wall for a little while, reaching the rope I had placed there earlier. I climbed down and took up the picket ropes for my horses. I led them back to the wagon I had found for them, and re-hitched the pair to it. The spring air made everything seem new again, and I couldn't help but feel like we had a much better chance against the world now.

"Hey, there! Step to!" I called out, snapping the reins. "Move on, ladies, we've got a job to get to."

CHAPTER 63

Two weeks earlier:

"I know the city's gone, Goddammit!" Vega screamed into the phone. "No, I have no idea where the hell they all came from. The wall is intact around Chicago! It is intact! I need more men here!"

The command center had been a nightmare from yesterday until today. Reports were coming in from all over the place that Trippers were ravaging towns and moving out into the country. The virus was reportedly moving faster than it had been in its earliest version, turning people into Trippers within hours. Vega had heard the reports of the Trippers eating their prey, but he hadn't believed it until he had seen three of them tear apart one of his men at the gate.

Vega grabbed another ringing phone. "Christ, what now?" he asked. He listened for a minute. "Sweet Jesus, they're that far? Okay, try to set up some kind of barricade that can hold them. What? No, we may have to pull back from there. Grand Rapids, too? God. Well, tell everyone to stay in their homes and stay quiet. What? No. I don't know. Build a wall, I guess."

Captain Vega slumped in his chair. His worst nightmare had come true. The Trippers had broken out of their pen and they were slaughtering everything they came across. The army was fighting, but they were losing in places and they couldn't contain the disaster. The government was dealing with full panic on the eastern side of the country while the western side was preparing for battle.

At least they have some warning, Vega thought. His mind drifted back to the trip he took into the infected country, and wondered if he or the men he came out with had carried the virus somehow, something they might have touched. But the first reports came from the north, not where he had crossed, so it wasn't making sense.

Of the woman he had killed or the man he had chased, he didn't think about at all. She was dead and he was behind a wall. If he came back over here, his face was posted everywhere with a hundred-thousand-dollar bounty on his head. He'd be caught in a day. But the Trippers were here now and that was Vega's issue. Since he was in command of the containment efforts, everyone was screaming for his head.

"Sir!" A drone tech came in.

"What now? Jesus, I don't have time for this," Vega said.

"Sir, yes you do, sir," the tech said.

Vega cocked an eyebrow at the tech who stood unflinching at the door.

"Sir, I was going through some old drone files, and you need to see this," he said.

"What is it?"

"An image, sir, captured by a drone about two weeks ago."

"Two weeks? What took so long?" Vega asked.

"The tech who was flying it took ill and we just got around to getting the files up. We've been busy, sir," the tech said.

"All right, here, use my computer," Vega said.

The technician plugged a flash drive into the side of the computer and pulled up the video files. The picture was dark, and it showed very little, until it came to a spot where the drone showed a man standing on the wall. The drone came in for a closer look, and the man held up a small sign with one hand. In the other, Vega saw him holding a small object.

"What the hell?" Vega asked.

"Let me zoom in, sir. It took some time for the resolution to get adjusted. But you need to see this, sir."

The screen blurred, and then the picture got clearer, zooming in. It blurred again, then it cleared. When it was legible, Vega found himself staring at the man he had chased on the other side of the wall. The man whose horse he had killed. The man whose woman he himself had shot.

The young man was holding one of the controllers the tracking teams used to open the gates in the wall. The other thing he was holding was a note, and it read very clearly:

Captain Vega-
You killed my world.
Now I'm killing yours.
You should have left me alone.
J. Andrews.

The technician left the flash drive where it was and exited the room. Captain Vega read the note over and over again. He didn't hear the phone ringing, didn't hear the alarm sounding. All he could do was stare at the screen.

He didn't hear the screams and gunshots, and he didn't hear the wheezing of the Trippers as they crowded into his office. The only thing Captain Vega heard was the sound of his own screams as the Trippers tore him apart.

THE END

 SEVEREDPRESS

CHECK OUT OTHER GREAT ZOMBIE NOVELS

900 MILES
by S. Johnathan Davis

John is a killer, but that wasn't his day job before the Apocalypse.

In a harrowing 900 mile race against time to get to his wife
just as the dead begin to rise, John, a business man trapped
in New York, soon learns that the zombies are the least of
his worries, as he sees first-hand the horror of what man is
capable of with no rules, no consequences and death at
every turn.

Teaming up with an ex-army pilot named Kyle, they escape
New York only to stumble across a man who says that he
has the key to a rumored underground stronghold called
Avalon..... Will they find safety? Will they make it to Johns
wife before it's too late?

Get ready to follow John and Kyle in this fast paced thriller
that mixes zombie horror with gladiator style arena action!

WHITE FLAG OF THE DEAD
by Joseph Talluto

Millions died when the Enillo Virus swept the earth. Millions more were lost when the victims of the plague
refused to stay dead, instead rising to slaughter and feed
on those left alive. For survivors like John Talon and his
son Jake, they are faced with a choice: Do they submit to
the dead, raising the white flag of surrender? Or do they
find the will to fight, to try and hang on to the last shreds
or humanity?

CHECK OUT OTHER GREAT ZOMBIE NOVELS

Z BURBIA
by Jake Bible

Whispering Pines is a classic, quiet, private American subdivision on the edge of Asheville, NC, set in the pristine Blue Ridge Mountains. Which is good since the zombie apocalypse has come to Western North Carolina and really put suburban living to the test!

Surrounded by a sea of the undead, the residents of Whispering Pines have adapted their bucolic life of block parties to scavenging parties, common area groundskeeping to immediate area warfare, neighborhood beautification to neighborhood fortification.

But, even in the best of times, suburban living has its ups and downs what with nosy neighbors, a strict Home Owners' Association, and a property management company that believes the words "strict interpretation" are holy words when applied to the HOA covenants. Now with the zombie apocalypse upon them even those innocuous, daily irritations quickly become dramatic struggles for personal identity, family security, and straight up survival.

ZOMBIE RULES
by David Achord

Zach Gunderson's life sucked and then the zombie apocalypse began.

Rick, an aging Vietnam veteran, alcoholic, and prepper, convinces Zach that the apocalypse is on the horizon. The two of them take refuge at a remote farm. As the zombie plague rages, they face a terrifying fight for survival.

They soon learn however that the walking dead are not the only monsters.

www.ingramcontent.com/pod-product-compliance
Lightning Source LLC
Chambersburg PA
CBHW032011170626
46807CB00006B/2753